Anitbeet Productions Presents

A Thug's Life Revisited

by Yani

A Thug's Life Revisited

Yani

A Thug's Life Revisited

By Yani

Published by Anitbeet Productions

Copyright © 2016 by Yani

This book is a work of fiction. Names, characters, places and incidents are products of the author's imagination or are used fictitiously. Any resemblance to actual events or locales or persons, living or dead, is entirely coincidental

All rights reserved, including the right to reproduce this book or portions thereof in any form whatsoever.

ISBN 978-0-9969666-4-1

Printed in the U.S.A

www.theauthoryani.com
www.anitbeetproductions.net

A Thug's Life Revisited

Yani

1

It was another long day at the office for Jamal. He was completely swamped with a few cases that he and his partner Dante had recently closed out. Earlier during the day, a young man who only gave him the name George, had given him a package. With the size of his workload, he hadn't had a chance to look through what was in the thick envelope. Jamal decided that he would put it off until the next day so he could get home in time to have dinner with his wife, Tiffany. Their two-year-old son was having a sleep over with Deisha and Maurice's two children so they could finally have some alone time together. He promised Dante he would drop him off at home first.

"Yo homie, you ready to roll?" Dante asked as he approached Jamal's desk.

"Yeah man, I was just finishing up," Jamal replied as he stood up. He threw his jacket on and was about to walk away from his desk when he remembered the envelope that was given to him by George earlier that day. He snatched it up and he and Dante headed out of the precinct together.

"You never checked out what was in the envelope that dude gave to you earlier?" Dante asked as they walked over to the parking lot.

"Nah, I said I would look at it tomorrow since I'm off. Dude was real secretive about it like it was some Mission: Impossible type shit. It was weird." He and Dante chuckled. Jamal took out his keys and hit the keyless starter. As soon as the car started, an explosion erupted lifting the car from the ground. The explosion caused multiple car alarms to go off and the blast knocked Jamal and Dante back into a wall. Jamal's ears were ringing and his head and back hurt. Dante slowly moved to his knees and looked at Jamal in disbelief. Jamal looked at him wide-eyed.

"What the fuck was that?!" Dante yelled. Other cops ran from the precinct to see what happened.

Jamal shook his head with a look of shock written over his face. "Your guess is as good as mine."

"Nah fuck this. You're looking at that file tonight! Whatever is in it, they don't want you to see it." Dante grimaced. "Here we go again with this bullshit."

Yani

Sirens from firetrucks and ambulances could be heard approaching the scene. A Sergeant from IAB stood in the window of the fifth floor looking down at what was going on. His cell phone rang.

"This is Rutkowski," he answered as he continued to stare down below.

"What's the result?" a male asked on the other end.

"Targets were missed. We'll get them though," Sergeant Rutkowski replied.

"That's not the answer we were expecting," the man on the phone said.

"I know, sir. My apologies."

"Save your apologies. Next time, be more efficient." The man disconnected the call and Rutkowski put his phone back in his pocket. He continued to stare down at the scenery as the fire fighters put out the flames to Jamal's 2015 Acura RDX as he plotted on his next move against Jamal Williams and Dante Smith.

"Jamal! Dante! You guys okay?" a uniformed officer asked as he ran over to them.

Dante grabbed Jamal by the arm and helped him to stand up. They both coughed as the smoke from the blast and the fire danced under their noses. The uniformed officer looked them both over.

"Holy shit! What the hell happened? How the hell did that car explode like that?" he asked before flagging the medics over to where they were. Dante and Jamal looked at each other without responding to the uniform's question.

"Tiff is going to be pissed. We just got that damn car not even a month ago," Jamal said instead as he watched the fire fighters put out the flames.

"Yeah, but she'd be more pissed if her son had to grow up without a father. Y'all can get another car," Dante said in return.

The medics hurried over to Dante and Jamal to begin checking them out. Jamal was so pumped from adrenaline that he hadn't noticed his vision was blurred. He mentioned it to the medic and told them he had a ringing in his ears. To make sure he didn't have a concussion they convinced him to go to the hospital. Dante climbed in the ambulance with him.

A captain came over to them and stopped the medic from closing the ambulance's doors. "What the hell happened, Jamal?" he asked.

Yani

"That seems to be the million-dollar question, Cap. I don't know," Jamal replied as he winced before putting a hand to his head.

"I'm going to need some answers from you and Dante. Cars don't just explode for no got damn reason!" the captain said angrily.

"No shit," Dante said as he looked at the captain coldly.

Their captain stared at him for a brief moment and then shook his head. "I'm going to send a couple of guys over to the hospital so we can get to the bottom of this."

"I'm sorry sir, but we have to get them to the hospital," the medic said to the captain. He excused himself and stepped to the side so the doors could close and the ambulance could get Jamal and Dante to the hospital.

"That was a fucking hit," Dante said angrily as the EMT wrapped a blood pressure cuff around his arm.

Jamal shushed him. "Not here." He glanced at the EMT who pretended not to be listening but prayed they continued talking.

"You know it was!" Dante hissed.

"Yeah I know," Jamal agreed.

"And you know why," Dante replied in the same tone.

"Yeah… I know," Jamal said again.

"You already know how I gets the fuck down. You come for me, I can go from zero to a hundred real fucking quick. They don't want D-Ball back in this bitch…" Dante ranted.

"Dante," Jamal said firmly. He looked at the EMT and then looked back at his friend. Dante closed his mouth and shook his head. He was beyond pissed.

The ambulance arrived at the hospital and Dante and Jamal were met with two wheelchairs.

"I ain't cripple, man get that shit outta here. I can walk," Dante said angrily.

"Sir," the nurse began, trying to reason with Dante.

"Please, he needs to walk. Just let him walk," Jamal replied in a very tired voice. He declined a wheelchair as well and let the nurses lead them to their exam rooms. They were both given a quick assessment and then told that the doctors would be with them in a moment. After the door was closed, Dante walked over to where Jamal was sitting.

"Open that shit," Dante said as he pointed to the envelope that Jamal was holding onto tightly.

"You really gotta calm down, man. Seriously." Jamal said in return.

"Calm down? Calm down. Nigga, a muthafucking car just exploded and knocked us back to puberty. Your car, my nigga!

That car bomb was meant for both of our black asses and you talking about some calm down. The fuck!" Dante said with base in his voice as he paced back and forth in the hospital room angrily. The floor squeaked beneath the soles of his sneakers which caused Jamal to wince.

"Don't you think I fucking know that! But snapping and shit ain't gonna solve nothing. We've been through this shit before, D-Ball. This ain't new," Jamal argued.

Dante laughed sarcastically. He couldn't believe how calm Jamal was acting as though shit exploded around them every day. "Gun battles, nigga. A bullet proof vest can solve that provided they ain't coming at us with armor piercing rounds or is a good enough shot, fuck around and pop one of us in the head. But a bullet proof vest ain't stopping no fucking car bomb! They blew the muthafuka up and you all calm and shit like niggas get blown up around here every day, B. Did you hit your muthafucking head? They just tried to blow us the fuck up! What the fuck is in that envelope?!"

Jamal shook his head and closed his eyes. He was trying not to be angry with Dante because his friend and partner had a very good reason to be as upset as he was. But he was tired, exhausted in a way that he couldn't rationalize in his head. And he was not in the mood to deal with Dante's rants.

His phone went off and he saw that it was Tiffany. He hadn't even thought of what he was going to tell her. He sent her call to voicemail promising himself that he would call her as soon as the doctors finished with them.

Jamal opened up the envelope and pulled the stack of papers half-way out before glancing up at the door to make sure no-one was coming. Dante sat next to them and they both looked at the papers.

"You've gotta be fucking kidding me," they both said at the same time. They both continued reading through the paperwork that George gave to Jamal, neither really taking a breath.

The door knob turned and Jamal quickly stuffed the papers back into the envelope. His mind raced as he tried hard to process the little bit that he and his partner had just read.

"Detective Williams and Detective Smith?" the doctor asked as he looked from one to the other.

"I'm Williams," Jamal said as he casually waved his hand.

The doctor came over to him as he looked at his chart. "You have a slight concussion, a few minor cuts and bruises. Nothing too serious considering what the alternative could have been. Take a few days off from work, get some rest. If you start having headaches or migraines more severe than usual, if you experience any dizziness or if you faint, if you have any nausea or vomit over the next 48 to 72 hours, come back in so we can run further tests. Outside of that, follow up with your primary care physician and get you some rest." The doctor then turned to Dante. "Same goes for you, Detective Smith."

"Thanks doc," Jamal said as he took his paperwork. Dante took his paperwork as well without saying anything. When the doctor left, Jamal's phone rang again with Tiffany calling. He hesitated a moment before declining her call, still not sure what to say to her.

Dante looked at him. "Are you trying to scare her?"

"No," Jamal mumbled. "I'll call her in a minute," he replied as he thought about something.

"What's on your mind, partner?" Dante asked.

Jamal shook his head. "Nothing much, I just need to ask the doctor something real quick."

"You got me on a ride home?" Dante smirked.

Jamal laughed lightly. "You funny as shit for that one. Call a cab, nigga. I'll be right back."

Jamal left the room as Dante called a local taxi service. Twenty minutes later, he left the room they had been in and saw Jamal signing some papers.

"What are those?" he asked as Jamal was handing the papers to the doctor.

"Nothing. I just forgot to sign some insurance papers, that's all." Jamal replied before taking a breath.

"Oh alright. Well the cab is here my nigga. I need to take my ass home. My girl all worried and shit."

A text came through on Jamal's phone. *"Babe, where are you? How come you're not answering my calls??"* Jamal looked at his wife's text message and tapped his phone as he thought of a response.

"Ran into a little problem after work. I'll be home soon. Love you," he texted back. He stuffed his phone in his back pocket as he followed Dante outside where their cab was waiting for them.

"I got this homie, hurry up and get home to Tiff. He can drop you off first," Dante told him as they climbed in the back.

"Thanks," Jamal said to him.

They rode in silence, but it was a silence that was bugging Dante. He couldn't understand for the life of him why Jamal was so nonchalant about the attempt that was just made on their lives.

"What's really good, Mal?" he asked his partner in a low tone.

"What do you mean?" Jamal asked back.

Yani

"You been real blah-zay-blah about what happened tonight. That ain't like you at all."

Jamal shook his head. "I'm just trying to wrap my head around everything, you know? I'm finally at a point in my life where shit ain't chaotic. Just when I thought I had finally gotten some peace, this shit pops up. I'm just fucking tired, man. I'm tired. All I wanna do is enjoy my life with Tiff and my son and I gotta deal with this bullshit again. Again. It's like it never ends."

"So what are you saying?" Dante asked. He felt like Jamal was quitting.

"I don't know, man. I'ma just enjoy my night with Tiff and tomorrow I'ma hit my dad up to see what all he knows about this shit."

"You think he might know something about…?"

Jamal cut his friend off. "This is Andre we're talking about. You saw what was in that file. It would be a big fucking coincidence if he didn't know."

Dante nodded his head. "Yeah, you right." They fell silent again as the cab driver continued driving them towards Jamal's house in Mount Airy. They pulled up in front of his single, three-bedroom home on Mount Pleasant Avenue and Jamal gave Dante a firm handshake.

"Watch yourself out here, nigga." Jamal said to him as he held his hand tightly during their handshake.

"You know a nigga'll never get caught slipping out in these streets." Dante smiled in return.

"Alright, peace God. Text me when you get in."

"Alright!" The cab sped off as Jamal stuck his key in the top lock of the house he and Tiffany shared with their son. He closed his eyes thinking briefly on what he was going to tell her. Before he had a chance to turn the lock, Tiff was unlocking it from the other side and snatching open the door.

2

"Jamal!" she exclaimed as she looked him over. He could see the look of worry all over her face. She then looked behind him. "Why was a cab dropping you off? Where's the car?" She stepped to the side so he could come in and then closed and locked the door behind him. Jamal wrapped his arms around her and held her tightly. "Baby, what's wrong?"

"The car is gone," he said flatly.

"Gone? Like somebody stole it?" Tiff asked as she let him go and searched his face.

Jamal sighed and sat on the couch before pulling Tiffany onto his lap. "No," he said as he shook his head. "Me and D-Ball were coming from work and I pressed the start button on the keychain. When the car started, it exploded."

Tiffany looked at him with a frown and then shook her head in disbelief. "Wait, wait, wait… what the hell do you mean the car exploded? Cars don't just explode, Jamal. What happened?"

"I don't know," Jamal said quietly.

Tiffany searched his face feeling like there was something he wasn't telling her. She then thought back to three years prior when they went through everything with his uncle and cousin being killed and how Jamal was targeted as well.

"No Jamal… not again."

"Babe… I don't know. All I know is some guy came to the precinct with this file that he was instructed to only give to me by a cop named Felix. A cop who I believed up until about an hour ago was dead, but apparently he's alive. Very alive and my father is working with him…"

"Andre is caught up in this mess again, too?" Tiffany asked loudly.

"Babe, calm down."

"Nah babe, cause see when your dad comes around, bullets and death seem to follow behind him. I mean, isn't that the nickname Dante gave to him; Death? And let's not forget the knife wound I got."

"Babe, I didn't forget," Jamal said.

Tiffany fell silent as she rubbed her hands across the back of Jamal's neck. She could feel the tension in him and moved his hands off of her waist so she could get up from his lap. She motioned for him to sit between her legs and she began rubbing his neck and his shoulders. "What happened tonight?"

Jamal sighed and closed his eyes, feeling the magic that her fingers were working on his neck and shoulders. He took a deep breath and began telling her what happened from the moment George gave him the package until the car exploded and knocked him and D-Ball into the wall. He then told her briefly what he saw in the file.

"I thought I cleaned the department out when everything went down with Kristoff. But that was just one isolated group. Apparently there's some wild shit going on in the department. Murder cover-ups, witness intimidation, putting hits out on cops…" Jamal said.

"Yeah… cops like you and Dante." Tiffany added. "Why don't you call your father and see what he knows?"

Just as the words fell from her lips, Jamal's phone rang. He leaned upward so he could pull it from his back pocket and saw that it was his father calling him.

"Speak of the devil… sorry," Tiffany grimaced.

Jamal chuckled. "It's cool, babe." He answered the phone. "Yeah pops, what's up?"

"I was waiting to see if you were going to call me but you took too long. What are you doing?" Andre asked his son.

"I was talking to Tiff. We were supposed to go to dinner tonight…"

Andre cut him off. "Talking to Tiff? Son, you were almost blown to smithereens tonight and you're chit-chatting with your wife like it's all gravy?"

"Dad…" Jamal sighed.

"There's a price on your head. The less you say to Tiffany the better, you know that. You know that! This isn't just you anymore, son. You have a wife and a son and these muthafuckas got zero fucks to give when it comes to taking out a target. Bitches and kids can get it, too."

Jamal looked at his phone with a frown.

"I'm not calling Tiff a bitch, 'Mal. Chill out." Andre replied as though he could see his son's facial expression. Jamal shook his head.

"Put your dad on speaker," Tiff said. Jamal shook his head no at her and she squeezed the part of his neck she was rubbing. Jamal winced in pain.

"Alright, woman!" he grimaced. Tiffany chuckled and kissed his cheek. Jamal put his father on speaker phone and held the phone up.

"Hi, Dad!" Tiff perked.

Yani

Andre shook his head. Though he liked Tiffany and thought she was perfect for Jamal as well as a great wife and mother to their child, he believed she had no business knowing about or being a part of this upcoming battle. "How you doing, Little Lady?"

"I'm fine. Just trying to keep your son safe and happy."

"Tiff, I know you love my son and you've already shown that you have his back no matter what. But this business is not your business and for your safety and my grandson's safety, it cannot be your business. Do you understand?"

"Jamal is my business. That makes whatever this is my business as well," Tiffany said firmly.

"Do you want to see your son in a coffin, Tiffany? Do you want your son to see you in a coffin? Do you want my son to see you and Jamir in coffins? Because he tasted that defeat before, I'm betting he won't be able to handle the taste of that kind of defeat again. And I don't think you or your son deserve that either. So again, this cannot be your business. Do you understand?"

Tiffany thought on his words which caused her to be slow to respond.

"Tiffany," Andre said with base in his voice causing her to jump. "Do you understand?" he asked again, slowly.

"Yes sir. I understand." Tiffany shook her head. Jamal grabbed her hand and kissed her palm as he waited for his father to speak.

"Both of you listen to me and when I'm done, take me off of speaker phone, Jamal."

"Okay, Dad."

"A call has already been made to your superiors with the Cheltenham School District, Tiff. You are officially on a leave of absence. Pack you and Jamir's bags, because you're going on a vacation," Andre instructed. "Get off of speaker phone."

"Wait…" Tiffany stammered bewildered by what Andre said. Jamal shushed her as he took his phone off of speaker and stood up.

"You're slipping, Jamal." Andre warned.

"How you figure, Dad?" Jamal replied as he began to pace.

"A hit was put out on you and your partner tonight and you went home to chit-chat with your wife. Do you want to die? Are you out of your fucking mind? And then you start telling her about what was in the file like they won't tap your shit to see what you know. What the fuck were you thinking?" Andre scolded.

"I wasn't…" Jamal started.

"That's right, you weren't thinking." Andre cut him off. He blew out air as he tried to calm himself. "You cannot involve her in this."

"She's my wife, Dad." Jamal replied as he glanced at Tiffany.

"You CANNOT involve her in this. Be ready in ten minutes. I'm on my way. We've already been on the phone too long." Andre disconnected the call and Jamal closed his eyes.

"I'm not leaving you," Tiffany said as she stood up.

"You are," Jamal replied.

"Jamal…"

"Tiff!" Jamal said loudly making her jump. He had never raised his voice at her before. She looked at him as though he had lost his mind. "I can't do this with you and my son here. I can't do this if I'm constantly worried about you, if I'm constantly worried about him."

"We've been through this before," Tiff argued.

"Yeah and you almost died."

"But I didn't."

"You think because you shot a couple niggas, that you a gangsta now, is that it?"

"No, I'm not saying that. But Jamal, haven't you learned anything yet? Hiding me and Jamir away is not the answer. It didn't work with Tamera and your brother…"

Jamal looked at her with fire in his eyes. "Don't," he said coldly. "You pulled that card last time and I listened to you. You almost got killed. It's not just you this time. It's Jamir too, and I will not put him at risk because you think you have to be this ride or die chick. I don't need you to be my ride or die chick. I need you to be my wife and a mother to Jamir."

"I am your wife and a mother to our son, what are you talking about?!" Tiffany argued.

"Then don't fight me on this, Tiff." Jamal said loudly, silencing her.

They stared at each other for a moment before Tiffany finally gave in. As much as her gut told her not to leave him, he was her husband and she believed he knew best, so she submitted to him. Jamal put his arms around her and held her tightly.

"I love you, Tiff. I don't want anything to happen to you or our son."

"I love you too, babe." Tiff replied back. They held each other a little longer just listening to one another breathe. Finally, Jamal let her go.

Yani

"Go grab some things for you and 'Mir real quick. Dad will be here in a few minutes," he instructed her.

"Okay," Tiffany replied quietly before heading upstairs to their bedrooms. She grabbed a Louie Vutton duffle bag and threw a few pairs of jeans, shirts and lounge-wear inside along with her under clothes and personal items. She was about to walk out of their bedroom when she saw a picture of her and Jamal on the mirror. His arms were around her and he was nibbling on her cheek while she laughed. The moment was so perfect. She pulled the picture from the mirror and stared at it for a while longer. She then heard the doorbell and knew that had to be Andre so she rushed to Jamir's bedroom and grabbed some of his clothes along with his favorite stuffed froggy and a couple of bedtime stories that he liked.

"Tiff, we gotta roll babe, come on." Jamal yelled up the stairs.

"I'm coming," she yelled back to him. She looked around making sure she didn't forget anything and then turned Jamir's bedroom light out before closing the door behind her.

"Where's Lil Man?" Andre asked.

"He's with Deisha and Maurice. They were going to let him sleep over so me and Tiff could have a quiet night," Jamal replied as he opened a small hall closet in the dining room. In the wall behind a few cases of water was a safe. Jamal opened it quickly and pulled some cash as well as a gun and two clips from it.

"I see Norman taught you well," Andre smirked remembering the similar set up in his deceased brother's home.

"Hell yeah," Jamal replied as he quickly counted out five thousand. He handed the money to Tiffany. "No debit or credit card transactions. You understand me?" he said firmly. Tiffany nodded her head and put the money in her purse. He then handed her the gun and out of habit, she checked to make sure the clip was fully loaded and then chambered a round.

"Because a girl can't be too safe in these crime ridden times," she said, repeating what Jamal always taught her when he first began taking her to the shooting range in the beginning of their relationship. Andre smiled at her as he watched her put the safety on and stick it in the pants holster that she slipped on while she was upstairs.

"Alright, let's go pick up Lil Man…" before Andre had a chance to finish what he was saying, a gun went off hitting him in the chest. He fell back into the table and slid to the floor.

"Dad!" Jamal yelled out. Tiffany snatched her gun from her waist and began shooting at two men coming through the front door. One of them pulled out a sawed off shot gun and Jamal pushed her behind the island.

"Go out the back," Andre grimaced as he pulled both of his guns. "I'm okay, I have my vest on." He fired over the top of the island to give them room to run. The two shooters jumped back and ducked. One had already been hit by Tiffany's quick shooting. Though he had a vest on, it ripped through the side and he was bleeding profusely but still trying to go for the assigned kills.

Andre peeked from behind the counter and shot off a few more rounds. "Go!" he yelled to them. Jamal pulled his gun from his waist and they crawled hurriedly over to the basement door with Tiff heading down first. Jamal took a quick glance back at his father not wanting to leave him there when he heard Tiff's gun go off in the basement. The loud boom from her glock caused him to jump. He snatched her by arm and jerked her back into the kitchen. They were trapped with a couple of guys coming through the basement and the one guy left in the living room. Tiffany fired into the living room to give herself a chance to jump to the next wall. She dumped her empty clip and put another one in as she looked at Jamal. Jamal nodded at her.

Loud gun fire erupted from the living room as well as the basement. Jamal could hear cursing and yelling along with more gun fire and he closed his eyes letting out a sigh of relief.

"Pussy!" Dante spat vehemently. He fired another shot into each of the gunmen's heads to be sure they were dead and then stepped over them like they weren't shit.

Tiffany peeked into the living room and saw Dante's girlfriend Nicole tucking her gun in her holster. She walked over to Andre to make sure he was okay.

"This shit is like dejavu," Dante said as he came up the steps. "How many times have I saved your ass on some spur of the moment shit like this?"

"Don't mention it," Jamal said as he shook his head. "What the hell are you doing here anyway?" he asked.

"Shit, you might not think your car exploding was that deep but I do, nigga. Besides, you left something in the cab and I wanted to bring it to you. Nicole was driving her sister's car and decided to bring me. We saw when the two niggas shot through the window and peeped the other ones creeping around back. Nicole pulled her burner and said she'd take the front. I said fuck it, I got the back and we bodied them niggas. You ain't the only one with a rider." Dante said with a smirk.

Yani

"Good looking Nicole!" Jamal shouted to her before peeking in the basement. Dante had laid out four guys. Looking at them laid out in his basement left him feeling pissed and slightly scared. No way he, Tiff and Andre would have been able to take them all out and make it out alive. And what if his son had been there? He trembled in anger as that final thought crossed his mind.

"No problem, bro!" Nicole shouted back. She fixed Andre a glass of water and helped him into a chair as Tiffany dialed 9-1-1. Jamal snatched the phone from her and hung it up.

"What the hell did you do that for?" she sneered at him.

"Who do you think sent the fucking hitters, Tiff?" Jamal sneered back.

"Okay, but you don't have to snap on me like that!" Tiffany yelled. She breathed heavily, angry and close to tears. Jamal sighed as he tried to calm himself. He then grabbed her and hugged her. As soon as his arms were around her, she burst out in tears.

"I'm sorry, babe. I'm sorry." Jamal said softly in her ear as he rubbed the back of her neck.

"Our son could have been here, Jamal. Our son!" she cried hysterically.

"I know, babe. But he wasn't. Just be glad that he wasn't."

"Jamal, let me holler at you for a second, man." Dante said to his partner.

"Hold up a second," Jamal said. He reached in his back pocket and pulled his phone before calling his captain directly. He briefly explained what happened and asked for him to send specific officers and detectives to the scene to make sure no one random came. After he hung up, he checked to make sure Tiff and his father were okay before stepping out front to speak with Dante. Neighbors had already come out of their homes to be nosey.

"Jamal, is everything okay?" an older woman asked.

"No Mrs. Jenkins, but I got it under control. The cops will be here soon." Jamal replied.

"I called them also. Were those gunshots?" she asked trying to be nosey.

"Yeah. Thanks Mrs. Jenkins, but I got it from here."

She lingered on for a little longer before going back in the house.

"What's up, man?" Jamal asked Dante.

"You left something in the cab when you got out, man." Dante said as he reached in his jacket pocket and pulled out the folded up papers. "You signed a DNR? What the fuck for?"

Jamal took the papers and put them in his back pocket. "Don't worry about it, man." he said as he shook his head.

"Don't worry about it? Yo, what is really good with you, nigga? You got something you wanna tell me? Does Tiff know about this shit?"

"It ain't nothing to tell and Tiff doesn't need to know about this."

"She's your wife," Dante hissed.

"Yes. She's my wife, D-Ball. Just let it go, man. Let it go." They heard the faint sirens of the police cars and ambulances approaching, getting louder and louder as they got closer. "We need to deal with this shit for now and then figure out what our next move is. But we can't do a damn thing worrying about my personal shit. Let's get to Felix and this guy George so we can figure out what the fuck is going on before we're not so lucky with the next attempt." Jamal stepped out to the curb to wait for the first cops responding, cops who he knew were not the ones he asked for. He immediately did not trust them, but put his game face on as though he didn't suspect that the department were the ones who put the hit out on him that could have killed his wife, his father and his son.

3

It wasn't until almost four in the morning that Jamal, Andre and Tiffany were finished giving a statement about what happened at the house. Jamal couldn't believe how long they were keeping them there and to him, it almost felt like they were twisting it to seem like something illegal was going on. Jamal wouldn't tell them about the package that George brought to him. When asked why anyone would target him and his partner and now is wife and father, his response was "I don't know."

When they finally finished and told them they could go, Jamal sent a text to Maurice. *"Yo homie, I got a problem. Can Tiff and 'Mir stay with y'all for about a week until I can get her to New York with her aunt?"*

As they were climbing in the back of Nicole's car, Maurice texted him back. *"I just saw the news, man. Everything good?"*

Jamal thought about how much he should tell his best friend and then decided it would be better if he didn't tell him

Yani

too much over the phone. *"I got some heat and I don't want my son or Tiff caught in the cross fire, you know what I mean? I'll have D-Ball's girl drop her off in a half hour. Thanks bro."*

He was just about to put the phone back in his back pocket when it vibrated with Maurice telling him it was no problem. Tiffany looked drained and exhausted. When she climbed in the back of the car, she laid on his shoulder, falling asleep almost immediately. They took Andre back to their house to pick up his truck and then he followed them to Maurice's house to drop Tiff off.

"I need to take care of some things with my dad. While I'm gone, I want you to get some sleep, alright? I'll call you and Jamir later. If you need anything, send me a text." Jamal told his wife before kissing her.

"You need to get some sleep too, babe." Tiffany told him as Deisha was opening the front door.

"I will, I promise."

"And eat something, too." Tiff smiled.

"Hey boo. Damn girl, you look beat." Deisha greeted Tiff before hugging her. She mouthed to Jamal, "You good?" He nodded and she threw up a thumbs up.

"Chile, I am beat. Just let me stake out a nice piece of floor," she chuckled and Deisha laughed along with her.

"Girl hush, the guest-room is all set up. The kids are still asleep and when they wake up, you know Auntie Day-Day gon' run their little asses ragged." They went in the house and Maurice came out. He had grown his beard out a little more but his hair was still freshly cut and wavy. He rocked his Immaculata University t-shirt with a pair of ball-shorts and socks along with his Adidas flip flops. He slapped Jamal and Dante a hand-shake before throwing a "black power fist" up to Andre as he sat in his truck waiting patiently. Andre put one up in return.

"What's going on with y'all asses now? I swear you niggas stay in more shit as cops than when y'all was out hugging the block." Maurice half joked.

"Man these niggas done put out a hit on us," Dante said in a low voice as he leaned on the iron banister to their walk-way.

Maurice's eyes grew wide. "Seriously?" He looked at Jamal to see if what Dante said was a joke.

Jamal nodded his head. "Yup. It's a hit on both of us. And the fucked up thing is, we have no idea where or who it's coming from."

"They done blew this nigga's car up in the parking lot at work…" Dante added.

"What!" Maurice piped.

"Yeah nigga. This shit is crazy. Came busting through the front and the back of my house. God bless my pop's vest 'cause they hit that nigga first. And you know how Tiff get down. She pulled her burner no questions asked and started bussing back. My dad tried to cover for us so we could leave out the drive way but as we coming down the basement, Tiff had to shoot at niggas coming through there."

"Damn!" Maurice said as he shook his head.

"Yeah, good thing Dante swung back around otherwise we'd all be in body bags right now." Jamal finished.

Maurice shook his head again. "Nigga you got lives like a fucking cat, I swear to God." They all fell silent until Andre's horn snapped them out of their thoughts. "Well, Tiff and Mir can stay here as long as they need to, you know it's not a problem. Hit me up later and let me know if you need me to do anything else."

"Alright, homie." Jamal slapped Maurice a handshake as did Dante and they went back to Andre and Nicole's cars. Dante got in with Nicole and Jamal got in with Andre. He quickly sped up next to Nicole's car and motioned for her to roll her window down. "D-Ball, maybe your girl should head back home now and you roll with me and Jamal here."

"Alright." Dante agreed. He gave his girlfriend a kiss. "You good, babe?"

"I'm straight." She nodded her head knowing the less she asked, the better. He hopped out of her car and jumped in the back of Andre's truck before he sped off.

"So what's the plan, Death. I know you got one." Dante asked.

Andre smiled. "Honestly this time, I have no fucking idea what to do."

4

Jamal and Dante fell asleep in the truck as Andre was driving. Jamal felt like he had been sleeping for hours but it had only been close to two hours. They arrived in Jim Thorpe, a small town outside of Philadelphia. As he was pulling up a long, winding driveway, Jamal woke up and stretched. He looked around wondering where they were.

"Where are we?" he asked as he looked out the window.

Andre cut the truck off. "Out in Jim Thorpe, Pa. There's someone you need to meet. Wake ya homie up back there. You niggas were knocked out like two big-ass babies," Andre smirked as he got out of the truck.

Jamal reached in the back of the truck and shook Dante. "Wake up, yo. We're here."

Dante grunted. "Here where?" he asked without opening his eyes.

"Fuck if I know. Come on." Jamal got out of the truck and followed behind his father over to two huge cream colored doors with a large golden knocker on the front. Andre gave three hard knocks and then held a card up to a camera that Jamal hadn't even noticed. A moment later, George opened the door for him.

"Good to see you again, Mr. Williams." George greeted Andre with a handshake. He stepped aside to let them all in. "Hey Jamal. What's up Dante. It's an honor to meet you guys." He sounded excited as though he had just shaken hands with Stephen Curry, Kobe Bryant and Lebron James.

"Um, who the hell is this?" Dante whispered to Jamal.

"This is the man who's going to help save your asses as well as help find the muthafuckas who put the explosive in Jamal's car and sent the hitters to his home last night," Andre said as he pulled a Smart Water from a stainless steel refrigerator before sitting on a chocolate brown, leather sofa.

"Hi, I'm George. But you can call me G-Money. Or just "G", not for George though, for genius 'cause I'm a muthafuckin-"

"Knuckle-head," Felix said as he descended a flight of stairs. "Boy, sit your wanna be gangsta ass down somewhere. You know you not about that life."

Yani

George let out a goofy giggle and took a seat at a table that had multiple monitors. Jamal looked around at the room they were in which looked like a computer hacker's dream playground. There were flat screen computer monitors everywhere with file cabinets holding equipment Jamal had never seen before. There were also crates filled with books and files throughout the area they were in. He suspected that this was no ordinary hide-out.

Felix stopped at the bottom of the stairs and looked at Jamal and Dante. Dante was too tired to give a shit about who he was and why they were there. But Jamal looked at him with contempt and Felix could sense it. George and Andre could feel the tension coming from Jamal as well.

"It's a pleasure to meet you, Detective Williams." Felix said to him.

"I can't say the same," Jamal replied as he continued to stare at him. Felix nodded his head respectfully. "I wish I could say I was impressed, but seeing as though my dad faked his death for more than twenty years before anybody really knew, the shit is getting a little played out. Not to mention the shit you pulled put me, my partner, my wife and my son in fucking danger. So no, I can't say the same." With those words, Jamal stood up as though he was about to break Felix's neck.

Andre stood up as well and stepped close to him. "Jamal…" he started.

Jamal shook his head. "Nah, I had the fucking Russian Mob, drug dealers, my own fucking cousin, and the same cops who took the same fucking oath I took coming for my ass, guns blazing. I ain't go hide away in some fucking ducky spot. What the fuck is your excuse?"

Felix waited a moment before saying anything. "You think I chose to do this? Don't be so quick to jump to conclusions. I didn't choose this shit. It chose me. I planned on coming back when I recovered from my injuries out in ATL. George did some digging when I told him if anything happened to me to give the package I had to you and Dante. He wanted to know why I chose you and that's how he came across Andre. George approached your dad and told him there was a potential threat against you. They started digging together after George showed him what he found. What I had at the time was NOTHING compared to what George found and what your father found also. All I had was some small bullshit info; suspicions about my partner helping to not only cover up a couple of murders, but helping to carry them out as well, with a *hunch* that my lieutenant was backing him up. That was nothing! Why did I choose you to give that info over to in case they smoked my ass while trying to find Vanessa? Because you had already cleaned house. I figured if you did it once, you could do it again. But see there's some things you don't know about Kristoff and all the house cleaning you did from bullshit beat cops all the way up to judges and city council officials. Nothing gets done unless they want it done. They let you get that done because Kristoff was out of control and if a few people had to go down to get rid of that bastard, they were willing to make that sacrifice. They were actually hoping you killed each other. But even if I didn't have George give you that package, even if George and your father didn't find the shit they found in those files, a price was already put on your head by your old Lieutenant in Delaware. They were just buying their time so it wouldn't look so obvious after you wiped everybody the fuck out. So check your fucking facts, *detective*. Your days were numbered long before George dropped that info off. If anything, I gave you the fucking heads up."

The room fell silent as Felix's words sank in. He was dropping some serious gems that Jamal nor Dante were prepared for.

"Checkmate," George said quietly.

"Shut up, George." Felix replied sharply.

"Sorry, boss."

Jamal shook his head. "Sheila put a hit out on me." He then turned to his father. "I thought you killed that bitch."

"I never got to her. Plans got fucked up when they pulled that fake arrest and took you to that warehouse where they killed Norman. I was a little distracted saving your ass." Andre replied before taking a gulp of his water.

"This shit is too much," Dante replied. "At least last time, I understood partially what was going on. It was basically a drug war with Kristoff trying to turn the Philly Police into his legal team of drug dealers and hitmen. But from the looks of what's in that file, this shit has nothing to do with drugs."

"No, it's not drugs this time. This shit is bigger than Philly. It's on a bigger scale than any of us can imagine. It might even be bigger than we can handle. But what's the alternative? Running and hiding? Trying to dodge every attempt they keep sending your way?" Felix said in return.

"Who put the bomb in my car?" Jamal asked.

"I'm working on that now. It's taking a little longer than I anticipated because the defenses their security systems have are masked by some type of encryption. I have to be careful with how I penetrate it to make sure it doesn't back fire and gives me up," George said as he was typing. He noticed it became quiet, so he glanced around and saw that everyone was staring at him with similar facial expressions.

"What the fuck are you talking about?" Dante asked speaking for all of them. Felix and Jamal snickered.

"Basically it's like an impenetrable wall that their security system is hidden behind. Ordinary Trojan viruses can't get through and those that can will immediately set off a counter attack to find the hack- me. Since hacking a police department's security system, cameras and whatever is illegal, I would be facing serious jail time," George explained.

"Okay so basically you need to hack without getting caught." Jamal said summing it up.

"Yeah, pretty much." George replied as he rolled a mouse around on the table top and then did some more typing. A side window populated on a screen with various script codes that began to move rapidly down the screen.

"Well can you?" Jamal asked.

"Psst, you must don't know my name," George said in a cocky tone. Felix shook his head. George tapped a few more keys and then did an Arsenio Hall fist pump. "I'm in". Several screens populated on the five monitors that he had set up where they were all gathered around. With having control of the digital security footage from the police station, George was able to back track to the time when he left the police station to see if anything happened between that time and the time Jamal's car exploded. He immediately noticed there was a problem between cameras three, four and five, which were in the park lot, and the rest of the precinct's cameras. A person was shown going into the parking lot who was dressed as a maintenance man but the camera's didn't show where he went or what he did. Instead it showed something else.

"Well, well, well. Fuck's going on here?" George said as he put the footage on the main monitor in the center.

"What?" Andre asked as he watched the screen for inconsistencies.

"Notice anything wrong here?" George asked.

Everyone was quiet as they watched the screen wondering what it was they were supposed to see or what was missing. It felt like they were staring at two pictures trying to find what was in one photo but wasn't in the other photo.

Dante was getting frustrated and was ready to punch the tech geek in the back of his fucking egg head. Just as he was about to voice his frustrations, he caught it.

"Hold the fuck on," Dante said, and for some reason, the day Kiree was killed five years prior popped into his head. He remembered the Bonneville that kept riding around the block.

Yani

"Either that red Honda is riding past more than once or the shit is looping."

"Bingo," George replied. He typed a few things and then enhanced the footage on the screen. He then traced his finger along the center of the screen. "See the tiny lines moving across the screen? To someone who's not familiar with video editing, they wouldn't notice them. But that's a sign the footage was edited and they cut out maybe a good twenty minutes of it which is just enough time to slip in, get the device in your car and get back out without anyone noticing."

"That's crazy," Jamal mumbled as he watched the screen.

"That ain't the half. I would bet that the traffic cameras and those of the local businesses were tampered with as well with the excuse that there's an ongoing police investigation," George replied as he began to type rapidly.

"You could still check them to see though, right? Maybe they missed one?" Jamal asked as he continued to look at the different monitors to see if he could catch something they may have missed.

"That would be a waste of time. My hacking skills go so much further than these surveillance cams," George replied before imitating the laughter of an evil villain. Andre burst out laughing.

"We gotta get this kid laid," he said. Felix chuckled along with him.

"Holy shit, this nigga just hacked Google Maps!" Dante exclaimed. "Yo, when we're done this, I got a little credit issue right now. You think you can work your magic with Experian...?"

"Ay yo!" Jamal said before laughing. Dante laughed with him.

"I'm saying, that fucking hospital bill from Temple is crazy. I ain't paying that shit."

George spoke into a mic instructing Google to show satellite footage of the parking lot at the precinct during the time that was missing from the surveillance cameras. A map of Philadelphia populated on the screen and then zoomed in to the requested area at the requested time. They all watched quietly as the same person dressed as a maintenance man walked into the parking lot and headed over to Jamal's car. Jamal was speechless when he saw that whoever it was used a key to gain entry to his car. George hit a few keys to zoom in and got visual that made them feel like they were sitting in the passenger seat watching as the device was planted in his car. Jamal was getting pissed.

Yani

"Run facial recognition on that bitch," Jamal said through clenched teeth.

"I'm already on it," George replied as he typed. A split screen populated on another monitor showing the person getting back out of the car. George rolled the ball to his mouse around on the table top causing the camera to change its position to see the front of the person. They couldn't get a good look at them because they had a baseball cap on and it was pulled down low.

"That's not a man…" Andre said as he stared at the person intently.

"Bitches can get it too," Dante said as he continued to watch.

Finally, the person looked up enough as they were trying to cross the street and George was able to get a snap shot of her face to put it in for a facial recognition ID.

"It is a chick…" George replied. "Kinda hot too."

"That bitch won't be recognizable after I get my hands on her. Her family gonna have a closed casket for that bitch, on God." Jamal said in return.

It didn't take long for facial recognition to ID her. Felix's mouth hung open.

Dante noticed the look on his face. "You know her?"

"Sergeant Nunez from Narcotics. I worked with her on a few cases before." Felix replied.

"She's a former marine with extensive weapons training. Served one year in Iraq and spent some time over in Saudi Arabia. She was building bombs and spent two years working for the bomb squad before being transferred to Narcotics." George said after briefly looking at her file.

"I'ma kill this bitch!" Jamal said backing away from the table angrily.

"No Jamal. They got your number. Trust me, they're not going to let you get anywhere near her. More than likely, she's on a paid vacation somewhere maxing and relaxing on a beach. I got this." Andre said to his son.

"Nope, she's not on vacation. She's working today. She just pulled up to the station and is heading inside." George told them. "I was able to clone the recording software from the Google Map's satellite and I have it tracking her."

"Damn boy, you are good." Andre complimented him.

"Can you do that anywhere or with anyone?" Jamal asked.

"Well yeah, but I wouldn't be able to do it for too long or with too many people or it'll set off all kinds of alarms and my black ass will be sitting in the basement of the Pentagon getting water boarded or some heinous shit like that."

"How many more people can you watch without setting off these alarms?" Jamal asked.

"One more might be pushing it, but I might be able to tweak it a little. Who did you have in mind?"

"My wife, Tiffany Williams."

"Why not have him watch your son?" Andre asked.

"Because Tiff will never leave my son. Watching her watches him, too." Jamal replied as he looked at George.

"Will do," George told him as he slid over to another monitor and began typing. "You better thank Fast 7 for that wonderful plot with *God's Eye*. I was able to make my own version of it except I call it *Hawk's Eye*. I haven't been able to figure out how to develop software that can track a person no matter where they go. But as long as they are within 200 miles, I can track them."

"That'll work." Jamal said. He waited while George did his geeky-tech magic. The *Hawk's Eye* was able to locate Tiffany who was still at Deisha and Maurice's house. She was lying in a bed propped up on some pillows, asleep with their son lying on her chest sleeping as well with his thumb in his mouth. Jamal let out a sigh of relief, satisfied that for the time being, they were safe. But he knew she couldn't stay there without putting Maurice and his family at risk. "Thank you," he said quietly.

"So what's the move?" Dante asked.

"Well I can't be seen, so the only thing I can do is stay here and be your set of eyes for whatever plan y'all decide to carry out," Felix replied.

"Yeah, Jamal since you're the target, I think you should lay low for a bit, too." Andre suggested.

"Dante is a target, too. You expect him to sit hiding out also?" Jamal questioned his father.

"Actually, I don't think Dante is the target. I think the hit is just for you and possibly Andre. Had they succeeded with the car bomb, Dante just would have been an extra casualty. But they're coming to your home and blowing your shit up, Jamal. I think they're just after you." Felix said.

"He has a point," Dante replied. "If they wanted me dead, they would've sent the hitters to my crib, too."

"So what's the plan?" Jamal asked again.

"Oh, the first thing I'm doing is heading to Delaware to make sure that bitch Sheila doesn't see the next sunrise." Andre replied as he went to a locker and opened it. He pulled out a duffle bag and unzipped it showing a shit load of ammo from regular .22 pistols to an M24 sniper rifle.

Yani

"I see Death has some new toys," Dante said with a grin.

"You damn right. And this baby right here," Andre said before kissing his sniper rifle, "has a date with a linguini eating guinea bitch in Delaware. Can you handle Nunez, Dante?" Andre asked as he looked at him.

"Oh it ain't no thing. That's a dead bitch walking." Dante replied. He looked at Jamal. "You good?"

"Yeah I'm straight. I'ma check on Tiff and Jamir in a couple of hours. Is there a car rental place anywhere near here so I can get back to Philly?" Jamal asked Felix and George.

"Yeah it's an Enterprise not too far from here. I can walk you," George replied as he got up from the table he was sitting at.

"Alright. When Sheila is taken out, I'll send a text saying *Sweet Dreams* to let you know that bitch is in a permanent sleep." Andre said to Jamal and Dante. He slapped Felix and George handshakes and hugged Jamal. "I love you, son," he said in a low voice.

"Love you too, Dad." Jamal replied before patting him on the back.

"Let's go, Dante. Can you get access to a car when I take you back to Philly?"

"Yeah, I can hit one of my youngins up. They'll cop something for me." Dante replied.

"George, access all security cameras around Sheila's home address and intercept it. Dante, don't make a move on Nunez until George confirms that all security cams around that area are knocked out as well. Let's move."

Jamal nodded at Dante as he backed away and then left with Andre. Once they were gone, he began to feel useless and thought of his wife and his son. He wanted nothing more than to be with them at that moment.

5

After Andre dropped Dante off in his old neighborhood around 26th and Jefferson, he made his way over to Delaware. Outside of the couple hours of sleep that he had gotten while waiting for the police to finish taking Tiffany and Jamal's statement, he had been up for over 24 hours. His desire to put a hole in Sheila's head kept his adrenaline flowing, so for the time being, he wasn't feeling the effects of the lack of sleep.

He was sure to park his truck away from Sheila's home. He knew that she wouldn't be home from work until after sundown which was perfect, allowing him to squeeze in a couple of hours of sleep while he waited for his moment to strike. He set the alarm on his phone for 7pm, pulled his cap down over his eyes and drifted off to sleep.

Andre stood outside of a hospital room trembling. His mind was telling him to push open the door to the room and step inside, but his hand wouldn't make the necessary movements to actually do it. He took several deep breaths, willing his tear ducks to stay dry, trying to remember the last time he had actually shed a tear about anything. He hadn't even cried when his brother was murdered. But the pain he was feeling in his chest and in his stomach was too much to bear.

He took a few more deep breaths, telling himself that he could do this and then with a shaking hand, he pushed open the door to the hospital room. The room was completely white and brightly lit with a hospital gurney in the middle of the floor. He could see that someone was laying on top and a sheet covered their body. He took slow steps towards the gurney, each step seeming like it wasn't bringing him any closer to it. After feeling like he had taken millions of steps, he finally was standing next to it and looked it over as his heart raced in his chest. He breathed deeply asking God for strength to do what he was about to do. He grabbed the sheet with the same trembling hand that was used to push open the hospital door, feeling the cold crispness of the fabric, before snatching it back.

Laying on the gurney with his eyes closed looking more like he was sleeping peacefully instead of being dead was Jamal, his son.

"NOOOOOOOOOOOOOO!!!!!!" Andre screamed.

The alarm to his cell phone went off and Andre jumped awake breathing heavy and sweating. He looked around frantically as his heart raced a mile a minute in his chest. He struggled to get control of his breathing as the visions of the dream held onto him firmly. He closed his eyes tightly trying to block them from his mind's eye as he gripped the steering wheel, telling himself that it was just a dream. After he was able to calm down a bit, Andre reminded himself of the task at hand. He grabbed the bag that had what he needed in it and made his way to the rooftop that would give him a clear shot of Sheila.

"Oh bitch, you are making this too easy." Andre said as he looked at her through the scope to his sniper rifle.

Sheila was lying across her bed on her iPad scrolling through her Facebook page with the window to her bedroom open, letting in a cool breeze. Little did she know, that wasn't the only thing that she was going to be letting in.

Andre locked in on her and pulled the trigger twice hitting her in the head. She slumped to the side and laid very still as the contents of her head spilled onto her iPad and her bed.

Andre quickly took the sniper rifle apart. He put it back inside of the bag and gathered the casings that were on the rooftop with him before quickly making his way back to his truck. He sat inside waiting to see if he heard any police sirens heading in his direction. After five minutes and nothing was coming, he figured no-one was home with her and it would probably be a few hours before her body was discovered. He started his truck and a flash from the dream came back to him.

He shook his head and pulled away from his parking spot, heading back home as though nothing happened.

6

"I intercepted and shut down every surveillance camera from your access point to I-95. You have twenty minutes to get there before I have to bring them back up." George told Andre.

"Alright. Good looking, kid. See you guys in a few hours." Andre disconnected the call and haul-assed to I-95.

"Andre is on his way back," George said to Felix and Jamal.

"Good. One down, one more to go. No word from Dante yet?" Jamal asked.

"No, not yet. You don't really think it's that simple, do you?" Felix asked Jamal.

"No, but it's a start. If they want me dead, they got their work cut out for them because I ain't one to go down that fucking easily."

"I hear you. But has it crossed your mind that this might be one battle you can't win? These men are driven by power and money."

"So was Kristoff and you see where that got him." Jamal replied.

"Very true. But this is a whole different level of power. Power that goes beyond the White House. I'm talking Fema camps, dismantling the second amendment to make sure that niggas without felonies aren't able to exercise that right to bear arms. I'm talking about the blatant disregard for the 4th amendment by our own with unnecessary stops, illegal searches, assaults and even killings to push the modern day slavery agenda with the private prisons being the new plantations, the criminals, predominately black, being the new slaves and the cops being the slave patrollers out to catch the niggas. And you see what happens when they don't catch one as quietly as they want to. And then there are the school closures where kids who are already in fucked up situations let the grumbling of their stomachs force them to do desperate things recklessly as a means of survival for themselves, their siblings, and their parents, only to get thrown into modern day slavery. I'm talking about the crooked cops flipping it to make it look like the good cops like you and me are the actual bad ones and when that doesn't work, they're killing us. This shit is bigger than us, Mal!"

Yani

"So what are you suggesting? Are you saying I should just pack up my wife and my son and run someplace else as if the same fucking shit isn't happening there? What kind of a cop does that make me? What kind of a man does that make me?" Jamal asked Felix.

"Taking the oath to uphold that badge was the biggest mistake either of us could have ever made. How the fuck can we fight for a system that was not set up to protect us in the first place?" Felix argued.

Jamal fell silent knowing that Felix was right. He thought back to the reason why he joined the police force in the first place; because of what happened to Tamera and his daughter. He believed the only way he could take Samir and his empire down was if he did it legally, because trying to do it the street way would have either gotten him killed or landed him in jail. And he didn't want to end up that way. But then he thought of what happened afterwards as well as during the time he joined the force with his Lieutenant, Sheila, and the crooked cops who were trying to kill him almost three years ago and now.

Jamal was never one to run from a fight. Before he would skip town and hide out some place, he would rather turn in his badge and change careers. He shook his head. "I need to see my wife and my son." He snatched his jacket from off of the chocolate brown sofa and headed towards the door.

"Jamal, watch yourself out there. Just because Sheila is taken out and Dante is handling Nunez doesn't change the fact that there's a hit out on you," Felix warned him.

"I got this. Don't worry about me." And with those words, he left out and got inside of the rental car from Enterprise and made his way back to Philly.

7

Dante still had strong ties to the streets and a crew of North Philly niggas that were down for him and ready to ride whenever he gave the word. One guy in particular named Sketch felt he owed Dante his life since it was Dante who put him in the back of his car and took him to the hospital rather than wait for an ambulance after he had been shot multiple times on the corner of 22nd and Oxford streets.

"Ay yo!" Dante hollered from the window of his cousin's black 2009 Buick Lacrosse.

Sketch recognized the voice and turned in his direction. "Yo D-Ball my nigga, what's good?"

"Take a ride with me home-boy, I need to talk to you right quick." Dante said to him.

"Alright, bet." Sketch replied. He slapped his friends handshakes and gave them pounds. "I'll holla at y'all niggas later." He jumped in Dante's car and they drove off. "What's up dog. I hope you ain't got me out here on some one-time shit." Sketch chuckled.

"Nah, right now I ain't seeing you on no cop shit. I got a business deal for you. It's worth ten."

"Gee's?" Sketch asked with a raised eye-brow. Dante nodded his head as he came to a red light and stopped. "Oh hell yeah. You know I'm about this paper, bruh. Let me know what you need."

"A hit was put out on Jamal. They put a bomb in his car last night and that jawn exploded when Jamal hit the starter button from his key chain."

"Yo, I heard about that shit!" Sketch exclaimed. "I thought niggas was bullshitting because I ain't see much about it on the news. They said it was faulty wiring or a transformer wire that got loose and caused the explosion, or some bullshit like that."

"Yeah, that was bullshit. They trying to get my man outta here. I can't go into too much but I need you to handle this Spanish bitch for me. Make it quick and make it clean. Can you handle that?"

Sketch thought for a moment. He had a few bodies on his hands but he never hit a female before. He then thought about the money and his loyalty to D-Ball and Jamal and shrugged his shoulders. "Fuck it," he said. "Bitches can get it, too."

"My man," Dante replied. He pulled over and went over the plan with Sketch. He then reached in a bag and handed him 5k. "I'll give you the rest once you complete the job. Don't do a drive by or no sloppy shit like that. Walk up to that bitch as she's about to go to her car. One shot to the head. Don't miss."

"Nigga, you already know I don't miss." Sketch said in a cocky tone. "I got a silencer jawn too. That bitch going night-night tonight."

"Cool. I'ma swing you back around the block. She at the 22nd precinct and gets off of work around 3am. This is her address." Dante slid him a piece of paper. "Burn that shit when you're done."

"You know me, canon. I'll roll this jawn up in a Philly and smoke this shit, no traces left."

"When it's done, just text me saying *This after hour lit like shit* got it?" Dante instructed.

"I got you, homie. I got you." Sketch said as he shook Dante's hand. He then got out of the car and Dante drove over to Nicole's place to spend time with her.

8

"Look who's here," Tiffany said with a grin on her face as she held her son Jamir in her arms.

"Daddy!" Jamir exclaimed. He squirmed out of his mother's arms and ran over to his father before jumping into his arms.

"Hey, Big Boss!" Jamal said as he hugged his son before spinning him around. "You been good for mommy?" he asked before tickling him.

"Yes," Jamir said with a giggle.

"You sure?" Jamal asked as he tickled him some more. Jamir laughed hysterically and Jamal laughed with him. Tiffany watched them with a grin on her face. He motioned for her to come to him and gave her a hug and a kiss. "Hey babe."

"Hey yourself. Did you get any sleep?" Tiffany asked him.

"I took a brief nap, that was about it."

Tiffany popped him on the arm. "Did you eat anything at least?" she asked him. Jamal shook his head no. Tiffany frowned at him. "You're so hard head. You're lucky I cooked a little something extra," she replied as she made her way into the kitchen.

"What did you make, babe? I am kinda hungry now that you mention it."

"I made some spinach and ricotta stuffed shells with chicken parmesan and string beans."

Jamal's stomach growled, his hunger becoming stronger as he listened to her. He sat Jamir on the floor with a few of his trucks and followed Tiffany into the kitchen. "See, that's why I married you, girl. You keep a nigga well fed."

"Oh? And here I thought you married me because I stay making your toes throw up gang signs when I…"

"Shhh!" Jamal said putting a finger over her lips and looking over his shoulder to make sure their son wasn't nearby to hear her. Tiffany laughed loudly before he kissed her. "Don't start what you can't finish. Fuck around and I'll get your ass knocked up again," he told her before nibbling on her neck.

"You already did," Tiffany replied. She turned to look at him.

Jamal stared back at her shocked. "Seriously?" Tiffany nodded her head. Jamal kissed her deeply, pulling her close to him.

"That's what I wanted to tell you last night but things got crazy and we never got to it, but yeah. I'm nine weeks. I confirmed it a few days ago."

Jamal stared at her only able to think of how much he was in love with her. "You know my mom is going to be super hype when we tell her."

"Oooh, speaking of your mom. She called me earlier today. She is pissed. She heard about what happened with the car and then what happened at the house. She said she's been trying to call you but your phone just rang once and went to voicemail. You might want to call her and let her know you're okay. Shawn called, too. He said don't make him come all the way from Miami to Philly to… how did he say it again? Nigga stomp the shit out of you if you don't answer your phone and let him know you're okay."

Jamal took his phone out of his back pocket and looked at it. He frowned. "I don't see any calls from either one of them."

"Hey, don't shoot the messenger," Tiffany replied as she finished fixing his plate.

Yani

Jamal dialed his mother first but he heard a weird buzzing and static-like sound as though he was calling a fax machine. He hung up and tried again but the same thing happened. "Something's up with my phone. I'll call Sprint in a little bit and have them check it out for me." Jamal put his arms around Tiffany's waist as they walked to Maurice and Deisha's dining room and whispered in her ear. "You better be glad we not home right now, or I'd be tearing that ass up," he whispered in her ear. Tiffany burst out laughing.

"Daddy, can you get me some ice-cream, please?" Jamir asked as he tugged on Jamal's shirt.

"Sure, Big Boss. What kind of ice-cream do you want?"

"The green one with the chocolate chips in it," Jamir said with a big smile on his face.

"Alright, Big Boss. Let Daddy eat his food real quick and I'll run over to 7-11 and get your ice-cream. That sound like a bet?" Jamir nodded his head quickly and then ran back in the living room when he heard Tom & Jerry coming on the television.

"Where's Deisha and Maurice?" Jamal asked as he began eating his food.

"Deisha is hanging with Keisha and Maurice has the kids at his mom's house. They asked if we wanted to come but I told them I wanted to wait here in case you came by."

"Aww, you wanted to be here when Daddy came in." Jamal smirked. Tiffany smiled with him. She had so many questions about what was going on but knew it wouldn't be a good idea to have that conversation in front of their son. Instead she watched Jamal eat, loving everything about him. Jamal completed her and she couldn't be happier with being his wife and the mother of his children.

When he was done eating, Tiffany cleared his plate and passed him an Arizona from the refrigerator. He took a few sips before sitting it on the counter.

"I'm about to grab his ice-cream real quick. Wanna sneak in a lil something-something when I come back if Mar and Deisha aren't here?"

Tiffany laughed. "You are so nasty!"

"That's why you married me."

"Yup!" Tiffany replied before laughing again.

"Damn shame, you don't even deny it." Jamal kissed her briefly and then gave her a longer, deeper kiss. "I love you, babe.

"I love you, too." Tiffany replied with a grin.

"Be back in a bit with your ice-cream 'Mir Mir." Jamal said as he rubbed his son's head while making his way to the door.

"Okay, Daddy." Jamir replied with his eyes glued to his favorite cartoon on TV.

Jamal left out the house and went over to his rental car. Just as he was getting in, Tiffany's phone rang.

"Hello?" she replied.

"Tiff, this is Felix. I'm working with Andre, Jamal and Dante. We've been trying to call him but it's some type of interference with his phone. Is he still there?" Felix asked.

"He just left to run to the store to get our son some ice-cream real quick."

Felix cursed under his breath. "Okay. Was there anybody at the house today besides you and Mir?"

"Yeah, Maurice and Deisha and their two kids. They left earlier today. Then about an hour or two after they left, a PGW man came to check the meter. But that was it."

Felix became quiet as he looked at George.

"That wasn't a PGW man," George whispered. "Those meters are digital so there's no need to come out and do readings."

"Is everything okay?" Tiffany asked sensing something wasn't right.

"What store did you say Jamal went to?" Felix asked her again.

"I think he said 7-11. Felix, you got me kinda worried here. What's up?" Tiffany asked.

"I'ma call you back." Felix disconnected the call and tried to call Jamal again. The same buzzing sound as though he was calling a fax machine occurred. He disconnected the call.

"Get Andre on the phone and get D-Ball on the phone now! Now!" Felix yelled.

"Okay," George said nervously. He quickly dialed Andre first. "Andre, how far are you from Philly?"

"I'd say about thirty minutes maybe. Why, what's up?"

Felix snatched the phone. "Something's wrong with Jamal's phone. There's some kind of interference where we can't get through to him."

"Some kind of interference like what?" Andre asked as he began to weave in and out of traffic.

"I don't know. Every time we try to call him, it sounds like we're calling a fax machine. I just called Tiff and she said somebody was at the house earlier from PGW to do a meter reading."

"Sonuva bitch," Andre replied, catching on to the problem before Felix stated it. "I'm on my way. Tell George to use the

Hawk's Eye to find Jamal and then call D-Ball and tell him to get his ass to him now. They're gonna try to hit him tonight. Move, now!" Andre practically yelled before disconnecting the call. He drove faster trying to get to Philly as quickly as he could. Felix then dialed Dante.

"Yo, where are you?" Felix asked as soon as Dante answered.

"At my girl's crib. I stopped by real quick to check in with her and to change my clothes. Why, what's up?"

Felix told Dante the same thing he told Andre. "We think they're about to try another hit on him again."

"Shit! Alright. I'm on my way to him. You said he's at 7-11 not too far from where Deisha and Maurice live, right?" Dante asked as he flew down the stairs and out the front door.

"Yeah, that's what Tiff said."

"Alright," Dante disconnected the call and jumped back into the black Lacrosse. He sped off hoping that he got to Jamal before it was too late.

✖ ✖ ✖

Jamal pulled up to the 7-11 and got out of the car. He was just about to pull open the door to the store when two police cars drove up quickly behind him. He turned around wondering what the problem was when one of the officers jumped from the car with his gun drawn.

"Put your hands in the air, don't move!" the cop with the gun drawn yelled.

Jamal's confused look became even more confused. "Yo, I just got here, what the hell is the problem?"

"Hands in the air! Let me see your hands, motherfucker! Show us your hands!" another cop yelled.

Jamal's heart raced as he looked at the cops with their guns drawn on him. *"I don't believe this shit!"* he thought to himself.

He slowly raised his hands in the air. "Look, I'm a cop. My name is Detective Jamal Williams from the 22nd precinct. My badge is in my left back pocket. Let me just…"

"Gun!" one of the officers yelled.

Gunshots erupted hitting Jamal in his shoulder. The officers fired hitting him in his chest and again in his side. The gunshots rocked his body knocking him back into the glass door of 7-11 before he fell to the ground. He opened his mouth to scream for them to stop because he was a cop and didn't do anything, but his body felt like it was burning. As he

Yani

fell to the ground he felt a bullet hit him in his back and then everything went dark.

✗ ✗ ✗

Dante was two blocks away when he heard the gunshots. "No, that better not… I fucking swear to God. Please… don't let that be what I think it is." He pressed down on the gas and jumped a red light narrowly missing a car that was coming through the intersection. He sped around the corner and stopped in the middle of the street, being sure to pull his badge before he jumped out of his car. He left the door open, haul-assing over to the scene, his heart racing and praying that Jamal was okay.

"NO! No, no, no no…. GOD!! What the FUCK DID Y'ALL DO?!" Dante screamed when he saw Jamal laying on the ground bleeding and in handcuffs.

"Sir, get back!" one of the cops yelled at Dante.

"I'm a fucking cop!" Dante yelled back with spit flying out of his mouth. "He's a fucking cop, too! Awww naawww! Fuck is wrong with y'all, huh?! What the fuck… UNCUFF HIM, NOW!" Dante screamed as tears fell from his eyes. The cops were moving too slow for Dante's liking so he snatched the handcuff keys from the cop and proceeded to uncuff Jamal. Tears fell heavily from his eyes, blurring his vision as he sobbed loudly. He carefully turned Jamal over and checked for a pulse which was light. Though he was wearing his bullet proof vest, three of the bullets managed to get through.

"Come on, Jamal. Stay with me, man. Don't you fucking quit. Stay with me, man!" Dante begged as he tore his shirt off to put pressure on the wound that seemed to be bleeding the most. "Y'all just standing around, fucking do something! Fucking call the ambulance, what the fuck is wrong with y'all!" Dante snapped on the uniformed cops who were standing around. He reached in his back pocket and pulled his phone so he could call it in. He was so choked up that he could barely get the words out. "10-4 I have an officer down at 1003 Willow Grove Avenue. Detective Jamal Williams has been shot multiple times by fellow officers. I need an ambulance now!" Dante sniffed before placing his head on Jamal's chest, sobbing.

"10-4 say again?"

"Bitch, you heard me! I said officer down! OFFICER DOWN!" Dante screamed.

Sirens from an ambulance nearby could be heard and Dante let out a sigh of relief. "Hang in there, Jamal. You hear me? Do not let these muthafuckas win. You hear me? You hear me?" Dante said to Jamal as the ambulance began to administer first aid. As they were loading Jamal into the ambulance, Dante looked at the officers who had shot his best friend and partner with murder in his eyes. He had already made it up in his mind that even if Jamal lived, he was going to personally put a bullet in each and every one of them.

9

Tiffany sat on the couch with Jamir bouncing him on her lap playfully while they waited for Jamal to come back with his ice-cream.

"Daddy's taking a long time," Jamir said as he playfully smashed his trucks together.

"He'll be here soon honey, the store is probably just crowded," Tiffany told her son as she continued to bounce him. While he thought she was doing it in a playful manner, it was really her nerves. Jamal had been gone longer than she liked and the call she got from Felix along with everything that happened the day before had her nervous and worried. But she didn't want her son to pick up on how she was feeling, so she bounced him on her lap as she said a small prayer to herself.

She heard a key in the door and jumped up, almost dropping Jamir. She grabbed onto him and picked him up as she watched the door.

Yani

Maurice and Deisha came in with the kids who looked tired and sleepy. Tiffany threw her head back and blew out air trying hard not to lose her cool but she was two seconds away from crying. Deisha saw how uneasy she looked and took Jamir from her.

"Mir-Mir, you wanna watch cartoons in Mar-Mar's room while Auntie Day-Day talks to your mom?" Deisha asked Jamir with a smile.

"Okay," Jamir agreed. He went up the steps ahead of Maurice and the two other children and then Deisha turned her attention to Tiffany.

"What's wrong?"

Tiffany lost it and burst in tears. "Jamal left to get some ice-cream almost a half-hour ago and he hasn't come back yet. I can't call him because something is wrong with his phone. And right after he left, Felix called asking me some weird questions about whether somebody was at the house. I think something happened!" Tiffany said breathing heavily.

"Okay, Tiff, calm down. I know a lot has been happening lately but you have a little one growing inside of you and you can't upset yourself like this."

"Where is he?" Tiffany asked in tears.

"I'm sure Jamal is fine, Tiff. That 7-11 up there stays crowded so he's probably just in a long line, but he'll be back soon. Just breathe and calm down, honey." Deisha said to her as she rubbed her back. Tiffany tried to get control of her breathing but she felt like something was wrong. She could feel it all through her body.

Deisha fixed her a cup of water and continued to rub her back while she sipped it. Just as she was beginning to calm down, the doorbell rang.

"That's probably him right now. I'll get the door, you just relax."

Deisha opened the door and froze as she looked at Dante. He stood in front of her with his eyes puffy and red from crying, but she could clearly see that he had murder in his eyes. Blood stains were on his undershirt and he looked like he was shivering. She placed a hand to her mouth and shook her head not wanting to believe what she was seeing and not wanting to hear what he was about to say.

"Where's Tiff?" he asked in a shaky voice.

"No, D-Ball…? Please don't say it." Deisha begged as the tears began to spill from her eyes. Dante looked behind her where he saw Tiffany standing and looking at him with the same expression.

Yani

"Don't say it, Dante." Tiffany said as she shook her head. "Don't say it. Don't you say it, don't you dare say it!" she burst into tears and looked as though she was going to collapse. Dante grabbed her and held her tightly as she cried in his arms.

Maurice heard the commotion and came down to see what was going on. Dante saw that Jamal's son was behind him and waved his hand at him to take him back upstairs.

"We need to get to the hospital. I don't know what happened. And I don't want to tell what I saw when I got there while his son is in the house. But we need to get to the hospital now," Dante told Tiffany.

"I'm coming with you," Deisha said.

"Hurry up!" Dante yelled at her.

"Mar, watch the kids, I'll be right back!" Deisha yelled up the stairs as she grabbed her jacket.

Maurice came down the steps quickly. "What the hell is going on?"

Deisha shook her head. "I think they just killed Jamal." She kissed her husband briefly on the lips as he stood there not believing what he just heard. Before he could ask any questions, Deisha was out the door and jumping in the car with Dante and Tiffany.

"Bull-shit," Maurice said, closing the door and snatching his phone from his back pocket. He called Jamal and got the same static noise as though he was calling a fax machine that everyone else had gotten earlier.

10

Tiffany was going off in the waiting room. She had already slapped one doctor and had another one hemmed up by his collar.

"I don't give a shit WHAT papers you say he signed! He is my husband and I said SAVE HIM! I don't give a shit what you have to do. I don't give a fuck how many surgeries or blood transfusions you have to perform. You better save him otherwise you're going to fucking need somebody to save you!" she screamed with fire in her eyes.

Dante grabbed her and held her in his arms as Deisha watched with tears streaming from her eyes. It reminded her of the day they were all in the hospital with Chanda after her brother had been shot. She then thought of Shawn and her heart ached.

"Tiff, he's DNR. They can't do anything." Dante told her.

"He signed that shit after his car exploded! He wasn't in his right state of mind! I'm his wife. I'm declaring him temporarily incompetent. You have to save him. Please. You have to."

The doctors looked at her with sympathy and one of them sighed.

"Ma'am, in order to declare him temporarily incompetent, you will have to fill out some paper work. Then we can proceed with any lifesaving actions."

"Give me the fucking papers then," Tiffany said as she wiped her eyes. A nurse came over to her and handed her the papers. Without reading them she quickly signed and dated them and then shoved them in the doctor's hands. "Save my husband, now. Now!"

"We'll do everything we can," the doctor assured her before hurrying back to where Jamal was so they could get him to surgery.

"I'm gonna be sick," Tiffany groaned before puking on the floor. Dante grabbed her and sat her in a chair. She placed her hands to her face as she leaned on her knees shaking tremendously.

Dante looked up and saw Andre standing not too far from them and at that moment, he truly looked like Death. Nothing needed to be said between them. Dante already knew what Andre was thinking.

Andre came over to Tiffany and knelt in front of her. She looked up at him with tear drenched eyes but was unable to form any words.

"I will fix this, Tiff. Believe me when I tell you, I will fix this," he said to her in a low voice.

"All I want is for him to be okay. If you can't guarantee me that, nothing else matters." Tiffany said in a shaky voice.

Andre nodded his head before kissing her on the forehead. He then looked at Deisha. "Stay with her. D-Ball, let's roll." They left the hospital and got in Andre's truck. He then called Felix.

"Tell George to pull the footage from Jamal's shooting." Andre instructed as soon as Felix answered the phone.

"He just tried. All of the security cameras from that area were blocked minutes before the shooting. We think whoever that was at the house claiming to be checking the meter for PGW really put bugs in the front and back of the house to listen to what was going on. They knew Jamal was coming to 7-11 and they set him up there." Felix explained.

"Okay, so tell George to use his *Hawk's Eye* or whatever that shit is."

"The signal is being blocked. We think they made us so we're packing shit up and leaving out now to go to the next safe house. I'll give you the address once we know everything is clear. But we have another problem."

"What?" Andre asked.

"Before Jamal was shot, it appears to have been some robbery at that 7-11. They're trying to pin it on Jamal and using that as the excuse for why he was shot. They are claiming that he reached for his gun and they felt threatened which is why they shot him. You know the same bullshit story that they always use in these situations."

"Yeah and let me guess, they didn't mention his name or that he is a cop," Andre grimaced.

"You got it."

"Fucking bull-shit." Andre said as he shook his head. "Call me when you get to the next safe house." He disconnected the call and tapped the steering wheel trying to think of what his next move should be. Then he thought of Keyona.

"Fuck," he groaned.

"What?" Dante asked.

"I gotta let his mom know."

11

Two Minutes Before Jamal Was Shot

A young teenager was coming from his girlfriend's house when he saw the cop cars speed into the parking lot of 7-11. Feeling nervous by the way they pulled up on the guy who was about to go into the store, he dipped behind a large oak tree and peeped out to watch.

"Oh shit," he said in a low voice while taking his iPhone out of his jacket pocket. He began to record when the first cop jumped out of the car and drew his gun. His heart raced in his chest as he continued to record making sure he got everything in view.

"Yo, they about to shoot this nigga…" he mumbled as he recorded. "These fucking pigs crazy. He ain't even doing shit… oh wait… he just said he's a cop…"

The sound of a cop yelling gun could be heard and then the gun shots followed causing the young teen to duck down a little as he continued recording.

"Oh my God. Oh my fucking God, yo. They just shot this nigga and he ain't have a burner on 'eem. Like dude ain't have shit in his hands and he was trying to tell em that he a cop, too. Aww shit man… what the fuck… damn, dude already on the ground shot the fuck up and they still handcuffing em like what the fuck is he really gon' do now…? Damn dude not moving at all, yo! Oh my God, I think they killed that nigga and he ain't do shit!" the young teen hissed quietly as he continued recording.

The teenager heard Dante's car come to a screeching halt and turned the camera in his direction, his hands trembling, scared out of his mind. He recorded up until Dante took the handcuffs off of Jamal and called an ambulance before he backed into the small crowd that was starting to gather, and ran home.

"Cyndrell! Oh my God, boy! I was just about to come out looking for you when I heard all of those gun shots! Are you okay? What the hell happened?" the young man's mother asked after hugging him tightly when he walked through the door.

"They just shot this guy over in the parking lot of 7-11," Cyndrell said as he tried to catch his breath.

"They shot what guy?!" his mother asked hysterically.

Yani

"The cops shot this guy. He didn't have a gun or nothing and he was trying to tell them he was a cop but they still shot him," he explained.

"He was probably lying. You know niggas will say anything to stay out of trouble," the mother sneered.

"No mom, he really was a cop. Another guy came afterwards and was screaming at the cops that shot the bol, telling them that he was a cop. Look, I recorded it on my phone."

"What?!" his mother said as she stood next to her son while his shaking hands went back to the video. He replayed it for his mother. "You better watch your damn mouth, boy. All that damn cussing!" she scolded him

"Shush mom! Just watch. See, look what they did to him!" Cyndrell said angrily. His mother continued to watch and then fear struck her in the pit of her stomach.

"Did you show this to anyone else?" she asked him.

"No, just you," he told her.

"Don't. Because from the looks of it, it looks like they wanted to kill him. Look how fast they pulled up on him. And you can hear him tell them that he was a cop and what precinct he was from and they still killed his ass. Nah, you didn't see shit. You didn't hear shit, and you don't know shit. Whatever the fuck they got going on in that department, I don't want those problems in this house. Now I'm wondering if that car that exploded was really an accident. That was probably his damn car! Yeah, get rid of that video and don't let me hear any more about it," Cyndrell's mother said to him as she went back to the kitchen to finish cleaning it.

Cyndrell sulked up to his bedroom and plopped down on his bed. He disagreed with his mother and felt like what he had could be evidence to put the cops away for killing another unarmed Black man. He was tired of hearing about them constantly getting away with that shit.

He found himself looking at the video again feeling his fear turn into rage. He then sent the video to his email, his back-up email, made sure it was in his cloud and then uploaded it to Facebook and Twitter.

"Look what these fucking pigs did tonight! Shot this nigga up in front of 7-11 while I was coming home but dig the move. Dude ain't have no gun and was trying to tell them that he was a cop too. They still shot him with the one dude yelling gun even though dude ain't have shit in his hands and his fucking hands were up! This shit gotta stop now, bruh for real. Fuck these pigs!"

He sat his phone to the side. "Sorry mom, but this time, I had to go against you. I'll gladly take that ass whipping," he mumbled to himself.

Cyndrell's phone began going off minutes later with notifications from people commenting on his video, sharing it and retweeting it. But when he went to comment on the video in return, he was unable to.

"What the hell…?" he replied as he tried to refresh his page. He tried to comment again and received a Facebook message telling him that the post was no longer available. "Oh this some bullshit…" Cyndrell hissed. He then went to his twitter account and tried to respond to some of the people who retweeted and commented on the video there but was unable to. "Yo, what the fuck…?" he frowned. He refreshed and went to his tweets only to see the video wasn't there. He then tried to upload the video again and saw that he was locked out of his twitter account. He tried numerous times to sign back in through regular twitter as well as Tweet Caster and was unable to. Cyndrell began to get a very unsettling feeling in his stomach. His hands trembled as he tried to go to his Facebook page and saw that he no longer had access to that as well.

"Oh shit…" he mumbled. Cyndrell began to realize that he may have stumbled across something more than just a shooting of an unarmed Black man…

12

Andre drove down the street in silence, no music playing on the radio, no conversation with Dante. He was trying to think of what to tell Keyona about Jamal as well as what he was going to tell Shawn, but couldn't concentrate because of Dante's sniffling and crying on the low.

Finally, Andre pulled over and put the truck in park. He tapped his fingers on the steering wheel.

"Why'd we stop?" Dante asked as he looked around.

"Because your sniffling is giving me the shits." Andre grimaced. Dante looked at him confused. "I understand Jamal is your best friend. But he's my son. MY son. There's shit that we have to do and it won't get done with you sitting in my truck crying like some fucking girl. Pull it the fuck together. He ain't dead yet. That's the first thing. Second thing, cops shot my boy. Your fucking brothers in blue gunned my boy down and right now, I don't give a fuck about a cop. I like you young-blood, but as of right now, you've got a choice to make. Are you Dante or are you D-Ball?" Andre asked him as he looked him in his eyes.

Dante looked at him knowing exactly what he meant. He reached in his pants pocket and pulled his badge. He stared at it for a moment as he thought about Jamal and what had been done to him. He then opened the glove compartment and tossed his badge inside.

Andre nodded his head in approval and put the car back in drive so he could head over to Keyona's house. He was glad that her car was out front so he didn't have to worry about breaking the bad news to her over the phone. He and D-Ball got out of the truck and walked over to her door. Andre used his key to get in and saw Keyona asleep on the couch. He quietly closed the door behind them and looked down at her snuggled up under a huge blanket that she'd knitted while she was in therapy after being shot over three years ago. She looked beautiful and at peace as he watched her for a moment before kneeling in front of her. He gently brushed the hair out of her face causing her to stir.

"Keys, baby wake up. I need to talk to you." Andre said softly.

Keyona opened her eyes and smiled when she saw him. "I wasn't expecting you to be home today. Had I known you were coming, I would have cooked something," she said to him before sitting up. D-Ball turned his back to her so she couldn't see that he had been crying. "Hey Dante."

D-Ball put his hand up waving to her. "How you doing, Ms. Keyona?"

Andre sighed as he grabbed Keyona's hands, squeezing them gently. He shook his head as he was unable to think of the words to say. Keyona could sense that something was wrong.

"Andre, look at me. What is going on? Is it Jamal?" she asked.

Andre nodded his head and then looked her in her eyes. "I'm so sorry, baby. I'm so…"

"No he's not. No he's not, Andre. No he's not!" Keyona groaned. Andre put his arms around her and held her tightly as she cried in his arms. "Not my baby, Andre! Not my baby! Tell me he's okay! Tell me, my God!"

Andre shushed her as he held her. "They're doing everything they can, but it doesn't look good. It doesn't look good at all."

"Take me to my son, now! Take me to him." Keyona demanded as she snatched away from him. She stood up and grabbed her jacket. Andre followed behind her and they climbed back in his truck. She immediately called Shawn as they headed back to the hospital.

"Mom, I can't talk right now. I'm on my way to a team meeting and then I have practice." Shawn said quickly as he tossed his gym bag in the back of his Escalade.

"Shawn you gotta come to Philly, baby. It's your brother." Keyona said in tears. It then dawned on her that Andre hadn't told her exactly what happened to him. "What happened to him?" she asked through sobs.

"Cops shot him in front of 7-11. He had his vest on but he was still hit about five times and three of them went through his vest," D-Ball replied.

"The cops shot him!? But he's a cop!" Keyona yelled hysterically.

Shawn's head was spinning. "Wait a minute, what? Mom, who is that talking? Is that Maurice?" he asked as his heart was racing.

"No baby, it's Dante."

"Put him on the phone."

Keyona passed the phone to D-Ball.

"Shawn, man it's bad. They put a hit out on your brother and they got him while he was going to 7-11 to get Jamir some ice-cream. They must have fired over fifteen bullets at him.

Most of them were stopped by his vest. But he got hit in the shoulder, once in the back, once in the chest and once in the side. I got there right after they'd finished shooting and they had the nerve to have him handcuffed on the ground after they shot him." Keyona groaned and burst out in tears as she listened to D-Ball tell what happened.

"Where is he now?!" Shawn asked.

"Abington Memorial Hospital. They were rushing him into surgery when I left with your dad. Tiff and Deisha are still up there. I don't know if anyone else came."

"I'll be in Philly in a few hours. I'm on my way now. Tell my mom and dad I'm leaving Miami now." Shawn disconnected the call and gripped his phone tightly as his stomach twisted in knots. He then threw his phone and began kicking his truck. Chanda saw him from the window of their mini mansion and ran out of the house.

"Shawn! Babe, what's wrong?" She grabbed him to turn him around and saw the tears streaming down his face.

"Somebody put a hit out on Jamal and they got him while he was going to 7-11. They fucking shot him over five times…" Shawn sobbed as he put his hands to his face.

Chanda put her arms around him and held him. She was at a loss for words. "Baby, I'm sorry. Oh my God, I'm so sorry!"

That was the only thing she could think to say to him. "Jamal is strong. He's made it through tough shit before. He'll pull through this."

"Cops did this shit to him, Chanda! The fucking cops gunned him down like he wasn't shit. I need to get to Philly." He pulled away from her and went to get in the truck.

"We're coming with you. You are in no condition to drive right now, babe. Let me grab Dre and Amber and we'll come with you."

"I don't have time to wait for y'all to get packed up." Shawn argued.

"Then we won't pack. We'll just go with what we have on now and then we can get whatever we need when we touch down in Philly. But we are coming with you. Jamal is my brother, too. Give us five minutes. Book the flight and call your agent. Let him know to handle whatever has to be handled."

Shawn nodded his head and got his phone from the ground. He began making the calls while Chanda ran in the house. Just as she said, they were back out in five minutes. The kids had zip lock bags filled with grapes and strawberries with a couple of coloring books and a PSP Vista for Dre and a couple of Bratz dolls for Amber to keep them occupied.

Chanda jumped in the driver seat and made her way to the airport.

"I just got four tickets for a flight straight to Philly leaving in exactly one hour. We gotta hurry up. I don't want to be too late. I don't want to get there and he's already gone." Shawn said trying hard to keep his composure.

"Don't think like that. Jamal will be okay, alright?" Chanda said to him as she weaved in and out of traffic.

"What happened to uncle Mally?" Dre asked.

Shawn and Chanda hesitated not sure what they should tell the kids. Chanda cleared her throat.

"Your uncle was hurt not too long ago. We're going to take a trip to see him." She looked in the rearview mirror quickly and saw that Dre wasn't going to press the issue. She then began praying that nothing happened to Jamal as she haul-assed to the airport.

13

Cyndrell sat in his room a nervous wreck. He initially was locked out of his twitter and Facebook accounts, but when he tried to check again a half an hour later, both accounts were completely gone.

"What the hell is going on?" he asked as he looked at his phone screen and his laptop screen. He texted a couple of his friends asking if they would search for him on those social media sites and all of them told him that they couldn't find him. He went from being confused to scared out of his mind.

Cyndrell looked up from his laptop and noticed flashing blue and red lights out front. He peeked from behind his curtains and noticed four cops coming to his front door. His heart began to race rapidly in his chest as his hands trembled.

"Oh shit…" he mumbled. He heard the door bell and crept out of his room, listening from the top of the stairs.

"Good evening ma'am. We're looking for a Cyndrell Matthews. Is he home?" one of the officers asked his mother.

"May I ask what this is about?" Ms. Matthews asked in return already knowing what it was about.

"We received word that your son may have witnessed a shooting that happened over in the parking lot of 7-11 on Willow Grove Avenue. We just want to ask him some questions."

"You received some bad info because my son has been here all night. He was nowhere near that 7-11, so it's no way he would know anything about whatever happened over there." Ms. Matthews said with a straight face.

"Are you certain?" another officer asked.

"I'm positive."

"We'd still like to take him in for questioning, ma'am."

"For what? I just told you he's been here all night so there's nothing you need to question him about."

Cyndrell backed away from the top of the stairs and slipped into the middle room. He had a feeling that the cops weren't going to take his mother's word and it would only be a matter of time before they forced their way into the house. He turned from left to right trying to figure out what he should do. Hiding in the house was out of the question because there weren't too many places where he could hide. He opened the window and slipped out, landing on the patio to the kitchen. He eased over to the side and leaped over to the neighbors raw ironed patio and used the railing and the banister to boost himself to the lower part of their roof before climbing to the top. He then began running, leaping from one roof to the other, holding onto his phone for dear life. He had no idea where he was going to go or who he was going to run to for help, but he knew one thing for sure- the cops were looking for him because he recorded the shooting.

Cyndrell leaped from rooftop to rooftop until he got to the last house at the end of the block. He was scared and out of breath. He looked around wondering what he should do next when he spotted a large tree in the back of the house towards the side. He took a few deep breaths and said a small prayer before he ran and jumped from the roof. He grabbed onto a thick branch and tried to wrap his arm around it. He lost his grip and fell to the backyard. He groaned in pain as he held his sore arm, grateful that nothing else was hurt. He saw a kitchen light come on and heard the back door unlock.

"Who's out here?!" an intimidating voice called out. Cyndrell scrambled to his feet and leaped over the fence to their backyard before hurrying down the street.

Yani

Back at His House

"Unless you have a warrant, you're not coming in my house questioning my son about a damn thing," Ms. Matthews said firmly.

"You guys smell that?" one of the officers asked, growing tired of Ms. Matthews uncooperative behavior.

"Smells like marijuana. Ma'am are there drugs in the house?"

Ms. Matthews frowned. "Hell no, there aren't any damn drugs in this house!"

The first officer forced his way into the house causing Ms. Matthews to stumble back, almost falling to the floor. One officer checked the kitchen, another officer checked the basement and two went upstairs. The last officer closed the front door so no one outside could see what was going on.

"You can't do this!" Ms. Matthews yelled.

The first officer tackled her to her sofa and yanked her arm behind her back. He put his weight on her, smashing her face into the cushions of the chair. "We're cops, which means we can do whatever the fuck we want. You understand that, bitch?" the officer who had her pinned said closely to her face, spitting on her as he talked.

Ms. Matthews squirmed. "Get the fuck off of me, you're hurting my arm. I'm going to sue every last one of you bastards!"

"And who's gonna believe a junky nigger like you?" the first officer asked before looking at the cop standing by the door. He let out a sinister chuckle.

The other cop pulled a thick bag of weed from his jacket pocket and tossed it to the first officer. "Oh what's this we found in here." He yanked on her arm some more causing her to yell out. The cop then pressed himself against her. "Damn, this bitch's ass is fat." The two officers laughed together.

"He's not upstairs," one of the cops said as he came downstairs. "But a window was open. He may have gone out the window."

"If he was even home in the first place," the cop who had Ms. Matthews pinned down stated. He reached onto her table and grabbed one of her slender nick-knacks and began pulling her dress up. Ms. Matthews squirmed trying to fight against him. The other officer grabbed her head and forced it down to minimize her struggling.

"Where's your son, lady? I don't want to have to fuck you up in here, and believe me, there's ways I can do it without leaving a fucking mark," the cop said after he was able to get her dress up.

"Fuck you! I'm exercising my right to remain silent you fucking pig!" Ms. Matthew spat.

"Feisty little bitch," one of the cops who checked the basement said as he watched from the living room.

"You have no rights," the first cop said before ripping her panties off. Ms. Matthews screamed for him to stop, but her pleas fell on deaf ears. "Shut her the fuck up!" the cop yelled to his fellow thugs. The cop by the door pulled his gun and put the muzzle of it in her mouth. Her eyes grew wide as the tears came and her screams hushed down to a whimper. She cried when she felt the officer jam her figurine deep inside of her.

"Your son is in a lot of fucking trouble if he doesn't turn himself in. He has something on his phone that we want. If he doesn't turn himself in within 24 hours, we'll be back. And next time, it won't be pretty." And with that warning, he jammed her figurine deeper inside of her again and again making her feel like she would throw up.

The cop got up and they made his way to her door.

"Thank you for your cooperation," one of the cops who had searched upstairs for Cyndrell smirked before leaving out.

The last cop looked back at her sorrowfully, tempted to aid her but was summoned by his brothers in blue. He quietly shut the door behind him and left.

Ms. Matthews lay on the couch sore, bleeding and sobbing. She reached between her legs and removed the figurine slowly before dropping it on the floor. She then jumped from the sofa.

"Cyndrell!?" she hollered out as she hurried up the stairs. She moved down the hallway quickly, despite the pain that she was in and burst into his bedroom. "Cyndrell!?" she called out again. She checked in his closet and under his bed but there was no sign of him. Ms. Matthews scrambled to her feet and hurried down the hall to her middle bedroom and opened that door calling out her son's name but he wasn't there either. She checked the window that was opened and screamed his name repeatedly hoping that if he did climb out the window, he was in somebody's driveway hiding. When he didn't answer and she didn't hear any movement, she began to panic.

"Where are you?" she screamed as the tears began to come. She ran to her bedroom and checked even though she knew that he wasn't in there either. She searched her closet and under her bed, but her son wasn't there. She rushed back downstairs and grabbed her phone, second nature telling her to call the cops. But then she thought of the assault she had just endured and laughed sarcastically. She put the phone back down and leaned into the wall. "Baby, where did you go? Why did you run?" she asked as she sobbed having no idea where she should look for him or what she should do. Her phone went off and she snatched it from the table. It was a text message from Cyndrell.

"Ma, please don't be mad at me. When the cops came, I knew that they were there because of what I recorded so I ran. Please don't be mad at me and please don't think I'm a punk. I don't want to bring you any pain so I'ma do this on my own. I love you, ma. I'm sorry."

"Do what?" Ms. Matthews texted back. She waited for her son to respond but after five minutes passed, she was sure that he wouldn't be. She fell to her knees and began to pray for God to cover her son in his protection.

14

Andre, Tiffany and Keyona talked with the doctors while D-Ball paced back and forth down the hallway from them. Maurice had just arrived after getting his mother to watch the children for him.

"Has anyone called Shawn?" Deisha asked.

"Ms. Keyona called him while we were on our way here. I told him what I knew as far as what happened when I got there. They shot that nigga and then fucking handcuffed him," D-Ball said becoming choked up. He took a deep breath as he felt the anger rising inside of him and continued to pace.

"D-Ball, you were family to him over the last four years as much as any of us. You should be over there, too." Deisha suggested as she continued to console Maurice.

D-Ball shook his head. "No, I'll wait until they finish talking to Andre and Ms. Keyona." He paced some more glancing back towards where they were talking to see if he could get an idea as to whether or not there was good news or bad news. "Notice none of our so called brothers in blue are up here to show support," he said vehemently.

"Because they fucking guilty after what they did. They know they fucked up. How they thought that shit was going to go unchecked after Jamal received all that recognition for cleaning up the department like that," Maurice replied with a sniff.

"Andre told the doctors he didn't want any cops visiting or sitting in the waiting room. A few of them showed up and were turned away." Deisha said.

"Fuck em," D-Ball spat. "Fuck all of em! Fuck them pigs!" His phone rang and he saw that it was Felix. "What?!" he answered angrily.

"We got a lead on Jamal's shooting," Felix said to him, trying to ignore D-Ball's pissy attitude.

"What kind of lead? I thought you said that *Hawk's Eye* shit wasn't working and all the security cameras were blacked out right before the shooting?" D-Ball asked as he stopped pacing.

Felix put his phone on speaker so George could better explain what they came across.

"D-Ball!" George called out.

"Yeah?"

"I sent the word out to my tech friends for help to find any footage of Jamal's shooting just in case we missed something. Some kid recorded the entire shooting on his cell phone. He uploaded it to twitter and Facebook. That's the good news."

D-Ball let out a sigh of relief. "Okay, what's the bad news?"

"Somebody had that shit erased completely from social media. It was shared over 50 times and received almost 100 retweets before it was all wiped. However, there's more good news." George replied.

"I don't have time for the fucking cliff-hangers nigga, tell me what the fuck is up," D-Ball practically growled.

George winced and cleared his throat. "My bad, homie. The teenager who recorded the footage name is Cyndrell Matthews. The cops came to his house and did a real number on his mom. He fled the scene and is on the run. But he's just a kid so there aren't many places that he can hide before the cops finally get a hold of him."

"Wait…" Felix interrupted him. He turned the volume up on a TV he was watching. "The news is saying that Jamal was a victim of mistaken identity and are naming Cyndrell Matthews as a person of interest. They're gonna kill this kid if we don't find him first."

"How old is he?" D-Ball asked.

Yani

"One second," George replied before typing something on his computer. "He's 16. I'm going to try to hack into the security cameras in that neighborhood to see if I can get a beat on him and update you from there."

"You do that," D-Ball said before disconnecting the call.

"Who was that?" Deisha asked.

"A guy that we were working with that was giving us some information," D-Ball replied vaguely. He looked up the hall and saw the doctors shake Andre and Keyona's hand. Andre then waved him over to them. Maurice and Deisha followed behind him.

Andre had his arm around Keyona as she had her head resting on his shoulder, crying silently. They stood in front of them waiting for an update. Andre didn't know what to say to them so Keyona spoke.

"It's not good," Keyona replied as she shook her head. "They were able to remove the bullets but there was a lot of internal damage. He's going to need another surgery but they are waiting for him to stabilize before they go back in. He's critical…" she trailed off becoming choked up.

"They don't expect him to make it through the night," Andre said solemnly.

Maurice looked away and shook his head. Deisha rubbed her hand across his neck to soothe him and held D-Ball's hand.

"Any news?" Andre asked D-Ball.

"Yeah, I just got a call with an update. But if you want to stay here with Jamal while I go handle some things…" D-Ball suggested.

"No. It's nothing I can do except sit and wait and I can't do that," Andre said as he let Keyona go.

"It'll be good for him knowing that we're here for him showing him our love and support," Keyona reasoned.

"It'll be good for him knowing that we're out here catching the muthafuckas that put him here in the first place," Andre argued.

"When are you going to get it that a problem can't be solved by putting a bullet in somebody's head?" Keyona said. "All this violence does nothing except have more mothers in the same pain that I'm in right now."

"What do you expect me to do, huh?!" Andre snapped with base in his voice. "Go out and pray? Get on TV and tell them that Jesus would want me to forgive them so I do? Beg them to have mercy on us po' nigras? These muthafuckas don't give a shit about that. While we sitting here marching, begging and praying, they're strapped the fuck up, armed to the teeth and it's Nigga Hunting Season. No, niggas been begging and praying for fifty fucking years and it hasn't gotten us anywhere except a seat at the enemy's restaurant, a ride in the front of the enemy's bus and a chance at a semi decent pay check while working for the same damn enemy! You can't have peace with them devils. The only thing they understand is war. Well, they brought the fucking war to their door steps the minute they put a bullet in my son and I won't rest until I lay every last one of them six feet deep even if it means you have to lay me right behind them. For my son, yes, I will give my life to show they picked the wrong fucking one!"

Everyone fell silent not knowing what to say to Andre's vow for vengeance. But D-Ball agreed with everything he said.

"I don't want my children to grow up without their father," Tiffany said softly. Keyona looked at her wide-eyed. "Jamir is too young to hold onto any real memories of his father and the one I'm carrying now may never know what it's like to smell his cologne while they lay on his chest and sleep. They may never know what it's like to hear his voice sing them to sleep or read them a bedtime story. If he dies, they will be robbed of having those memories. They will be robbed of their protector. They will be robbed of their father. And though they won't feel the pain as I feel it now, what I do want them to know is that he did not come from a family of cowards who *left it up to God.* I want them to know that their father's life mattered and we didn't leave it to the system to give him justice when it was the system that took his life. So I'm with you, Mr. Williams." Tiffany looked him in his eyes. "Don't let them get away with what they did to us."

Andre hugged Tiffany. "I got this. Don't you worry. I got this." He let her go and gave Keyona a kiss. "You call me if anything changes, good or bad." Keyona nodded her head and he and D-Ball left the hospital.

"How are we going to find the shooters without any footage of the damn shooting," Andre snapped as he climbed in his truck.

"Felix called with an update. Some teenaged kid captured everything on his phone. He uploaded it to his Facebook and Twitter account but not only was the shit erased, they shut his accounts down, too. George said the cops came to his house to get him and roughed his mom up a bit. He's on the run." D-Ball explained.

"Wait, so there's footage but from some kid's phone who the cops are trying to catch up to. Well we need to find him before they do."

"Same shit I said. George is checking traffic cams and area security cams to see if he can get a beat on him."

"We don't have time for that shit." Andre said as he started the car and began driving out of the parking lot of the hospital. "If I was a teenager running from the cops, where would I hide?" Andre replied.

"A friend's house," D-Ball suggested.

"Keyona's house." Andre said in return. "Call George and see if he can find out if this kid has a girlfriend. If he does I'll bet a crisp $100 bill he's trying to hide there at least for the night, so he can get some sleep."

D-Ball received a text message on his phone. It was from George with a picture attached. *"This is a still shot that someone posted on Instagram not too long ago. I'm guessing it's from the footage the kid recorded on his phone. But I enhanced it so you can see the cop pointing his gun at Jamal. I then was able to put him in facial recognition. His name is Officer Curtis Daniels. I'll forward his information to you in a minute."*

D-Ball read the message to Andre and then showed him the picture when they came to a red light.

"Dead man walking," D-Ball said as he pulled his gun from the back of his pants. "I'm low on ammo. Hook me up, Death."

"You know I got you. Let's find this kid and then fuck this city up."

D-Ball nodded his head in agreement as they drove to one of Andre's hide out spots to load up on ammo and everything else they needed.

15

Cyndrell threw light rocks at his girlfriend's window after hiding out in their shed waiting for her parent's to go to sleep. She had already seen on the news that he was a person of interest in the shooting and attempted murder of Detective Williams as well as the armed robbery of the 7-11 that happened moments before Jamal was shot. She knew it couldn't be possible because he had left her place moments before the gunfire erupted. She suspected it had something to do with the video he posted that mysteriously was taken offline along with all of his social media accounts.

She heard the noises from the pebbles hitting her window and went over to it. She gasped when she saw Cyndrell and held up a finger to let him know that she would be right down. She crept past her parents' bedroom and snuck down the stairs and over to the back door. She stepped out in the backyard and Cyndrell hugged her tightly.

"Oh my God, are you okay?" she asked him.

"The cops shot this dude when I left your house and I recorded it on my phone." Cyndrell explained.

"I saw the video you posted online. I was about to comment but then all of a sudden, the video was gone. I figured somebody reported it and had it taken down. But then your whole account disappeared so I ain't know what to think."

"Amora, the cops came to my house looking for me. I don't know what they said to my mom. I got scared and ran 'cause I knew them niggas wanted me for this recording and I ain't giving this shit to them. Fuck that."

"Come inside. It's cold." Amora told him.

"You sure? I don't want to get you in trouble. But I ain't have nowhere to go and I'm scared to go back home."

Amora grabbed him by the hand and pulled him into her house. She quietly shut the door behind them. "They got your picture on the news saying you're a person of interest in all of this," she told him. Cyndrell was unaware of that news.

"Fuck... fuck, fuck, fuck, fuck..." He put his hands to his head as he tried to think. "I don't know what to do. I ain't have shit to do with anything. All I did was record it. I ain't know they was gonna shoot dude like that. I thought they might beat his ass or something but they just shot that nigga for nothing!"

Amora shushed him. "Come down in the basement. That way if my parents wake up, I don't have to worry about you being caught in my bedroom. You hungry?"

"All that running I did, hopping from rooftops and shit, a nigga starving and thirsty." Cyndrell told his girlfriend as he sat at the counter.

She quickly grabbed him some of the left over fried chicken from dinner and a slice of carrot cake before grabbing a cold ginger ale out of the doorway of the refrigerator. Cyndrell followed her down into the basement that was complete with wall to wall carpet the color of taupe. African paintings and pictures adorned the walls giving the basement a family-room feel to it. There was also a sofa, a recliner and a 50-inch flat screen TV. She turned the TV on and turned it down low while Cyndrell scarfed down his food and took gulps of his soda.

"Stay right here. I'll be right back." Amora crept upstairs and took a thick blanket out of the closet before joining Cyndrell back in the basement. He was finished his food and had put everything in the trash. Amora sat next to him and put the blanket around them before turning the TV to ESPN.

"Thank you for having my back, Shorty." Cyndrell said to his girlfriend as they got comfortable on the sofa.

"You're welcome," Amora smiled as Cyndrell kissed her forehead. Cyndrell leaned his head back against the back of the couch and before he knew it, they both had fallen asleep.

They were awakened by three loud knocks on the front door. Amora jumped up and Cyndrell got up behind her. They could see from the bricked, glass windows the flashing police lights in the front of her home.

"Oh shit!" Cyndrell panicked.

"Oh my God…" Amora squealed. She knew she only had minutes before her father came to answer the door. She ran to the other side of the basement and struggled to move a cabinet to the side. "Help me," she said looking at Cyndrell. He ran to her and they pushed the large cabinet over some more as the cops continued to bang on the door. Amora knelt down and yanked a gate off of a vent. "I used to hide in here when me and my brother would play hide and seek."

"I can't fit in there. It's tight as shit!" Cyndrell fussed.

"It beats the alternative. Hurry up!" She could hear her father's footsteps coming down from the second floor. Cyndrell got down on the floor and back in as far as he could. Amora struggled to push the cabinet back in front of the vent and then jumped back on the couch, covering herself with the blanket. She listened out for what was being said upstairs.

Yani

"Sir, we have reason to believe your daughter may have someone hiding out in your home and he's a person of interest in a shooting that happened not too far from here," one of the police officers said to Amora's father.

"What's this all about? My daughter wouldn't be hiding anyone in our home. What are you people talking about? It's damn near 2am."

A second officer held up a photo. "Do you know this young man?"

Amora's father stared at the picture. "Yeah, that's my daughter's boyfriend. He hung out here earlier this evening but he went home a little after nine last-night."

"If you don't mind, we'd like to ask your daughter a few questions," the same officer said.

Amora's father looked them over but decided it couldn't do any harm. He let the police in his home. His wife stood by the steps wondering what was going on.

"Debbie, tell Amora to come down here. These cops have a few questions to ask about Cyndrell."

"Okay," Debbie replied. She went upstairs and opened Amora's door, only to see that she wasn't in there. "Ron, she's not in her room," she said as she came back downstairs.

"Calm down, Deb. Sometimes she watches TV in the basement. She might have fell asleep down there," Ron replied. The police followed him down into the basement. "Amora, honey wake up."

Amora groaned and stretched before pulling the blanket from over her head. She jumped when she saw the police with him. "Jesus Daddy…" she grimaced as she looked them all over. "Why is one-time all in our basement? Did somebody die?"

"Are you alone down here, young lady?" one of the officers asked as he looked around. Debbie turned the ceiling lights on so he could see better.

"Yeah… who else would be down here? Daddy, what's going on?" Amora asked as she looked at her father confused.

"Have you spoken to Cyndrell Matthews tonight after he left?" the same cop asked her.

Amora shook her head. "He was supposed to call me when he got home. Had me scared a little bit because right after he left, I heard gun shots. But I knew he was okay when I saw him post on Facebook."

The cops looked at each other. "You mind if we look around?" one of them asked Ron.

Yani

"I don't see the problem. No one is here." Ron shrugged. The cops checked the garage and the storage room, walking past the cabinet and not paying it any mind. Lastly, they checked the bathroom and a closet, all which turned up empty.

"No one else is down here, sir," one of the cops said.

Amora kept her poker face as she looked at the cop who was asking the questions.

"About what time did Cyndrell leave your home last night?" the cop asked.

"Um, it was a little after nine. Scandal had just come on." Amora recalled.

"And you said right after he left, you heard the gunshots. Was it five minutes, ten…?" he asked.

"More like two minutes literally. I mean the opening credits to Scandal were still rolling when I heard about fifteen gunshots."

The cops looked at each other again. "And how long was it before Cyndrell posted on Facebook?"

"I don't know… maybe fifteen minutes after that. I would be able to tell you exactly but his account disappeared," Amora said as she looked at them suspiciously.

"What do you mean *disappeared*?" another cop asked.

Amora shrugged her shoulders and thought to herself *"Fuck it"*. "Cyndrell posted a video of the cops shooting this man in front of 7-11. He said the guy they shot was unarmed and had his hands up and also that he was trying to tell them he was a detective from the 22nd district. On the video you could hear a cop yelling *Gun* even though the guy had nothing in his hands, wasn't reaching or anything. I was going to comment on the video but that's when it disappeared... or something." She looked at each of the cops with a smirk on her face. Ron and Debbie looked at each other catching on to what this was about.

"Okay, I think that's enough. I had no idea that this went on. I didn't even hear the gun shots because I was in the shower at the time. But, as you can see, no one is here and my daughter doesn't know where Cyndrell is if he isn't at home with his own mother." Ron said as he put his arm around his daughter.

The cop looked at him wanting to do bodily harm but was able to restrain himself and forced a smile. "I understand. Thank you for your help, Amora. If you happen to think of anything else or if Cyndrell contacts you..." he tried to hand her a business card but Ron intercepted it.

"You gentlemen have a good evening," he said as he tucked the business card in the pocket to his pajama bottoms. The cop nodded his head and they all left out of the basement. When they were gone from in front of the house, Ron turned back to Amora.

"Where is he?" Ron asked her.

"I don't know, Dad. I haven't heard from him," Amora said with wide innocent eyes.

"Amora, don't lie to me. If that boy witnessed an execution by cops of another cop and got it recorded, he's in more danger than you can possibly imagine. I saw the look on their faces when you mentioned what was on that video. He's more than just a person of interest."

"Dad…" Amora started to lie again but this time her mother hushed her.

"Amora, I know you care about this boy a lot. He's your first boyfriend and now-a-days you little girls think you're supposed to ride for your man. But it's not your job to protect him from this. You can't protect him and trying to could put you in danger. So if you know where he is, tell us so we can help him."

"Help him how? By giving him to the cops?" Amora asked her parents.

"We won't do that, we promise. But with my connections to NBC news, I can get his footage leaked to the news channels and help him that way," her father assured her.

Amora looked at her mother and father and sighed giving in. She went back down in the basement and they followed her. She went over to the cabinet and stopped dead in her tracks when she saw that it was moved. Amora dropped to the floor and looked in the vent only to see that Cyndrell wasn't in there. She jumped up and checked the garage, storage room and bathroom, but he wasn't there either.

"He's gone..." Amora said as she looked around. She looked at her father with tears in her eyes. "Dad, he's gone. I helped him hide in the vent like I used to before Assad went to college and we would play hide and seek in the house."

"Damn it, Amora." Her father shook his head as he tried to think. "You shouldn't have lied to us."

"I'm sorry, daddy... I just didn't want anything to happen to him."

"Call him and try to get him to come back to the house. Let him know we can help him," Debbie suggested.

Amora grabbed her iPhone that should have been charging and noticed the charger wasn't connected. She chuckled when she realized Cyndrell had taken it. She dialed his number. He answered after the first ring.

"Rell! Why did you leave? Where'd you go?" Amora exclaimed.

"I couldn't let you and your parents take the heat for me like that so I bounced. I took your charger," Cyndrell said to her.

"I noticed, punk. You better get me another one, too." Amora smiled. She saw how impatient her father was becoming. "Come back to the house. My dad said he can get your video on NBC news. That'll get the cops off your back."

Cyndrell thought about it for a minute. It was chilly outside and he had no idea where he was going to go. He then began to think that her father only said that to get him back to the house so he could turn him over to the cops and he shook his head.

"Nah. I can't. I gotta go. Thanks again for having my back Amora. I love you."

Amora froze. That was the first time he told her that in the five months they had been going together. She looked at her father and her mother afraid to say it back in front of them.

"It's okay if you can't say it because your pops and mom dukes are in front of you. But I wanted you to know that anyway," Cyndrell said to her.

"I love you, too," she blurted out, no longer caring what her mother and father thought. Her father kept a straight face while her mother tried to suppress her grin.

"My phone about to…" Cyndrell was cut off abruptly.

"Rell!" Amora said into the phone. She looked at the screen and saw that the call dropped. She shook her head and tossed her phone onto the couch. "I think his phone died."

Ron sighed. "Is he going to come back to the house?"

"No. I don't think he is. He's probably scared you're going to turn him over to the cops." Amora plopped down on the couch and covered her face.

"He'll be okay sweetheart. Just trust that God will look after him. But you need to get some sleep. You have to be up in a few hours for school tomorrow," Debbie said.

"Can't I stay home?" Amora pleaded. "Y'all know if you send me to school the teachers are going to be hounding me thinking I know where Cyndrell is. People in school are going to be all in my face and what if the cops try to question me again while y'all aren't there?"

Ron took a moment to think on what she said and figured she had a point. "Get to bed and I'll decide in the morning. I got a feeling Cyndrell won't be in school. Maybe if he knows you're here, he'll come back," he told her. They all filed up the stairs to their bedrooms and went to bed. Amora couldn't sleep however. She got her mother's charger and plugged her phone in hoping Cyndrell would text or call her back. She replayed him telling her that he loved her over and over in her head, getting butterflies each time she heard his voice when he said it. She checked her phone one last time but there was still no text or call from him. She finally sent him another text telling him she loved him again and to please text her to let her know he was okay before rolling over and falling asleep.

14

Shawn touched down in Philly a little after 3am. Chanda called her father to see if she could bring the children by so she could be with Shawn at the hospital with Jamal. After dropping them off and booking a hotel room, they managed to dodge the media as they made their way to Abington Memorial Hospital to see Jamal.

Shawn looked at Maurice and Deisha leaning on each other sleeping. He noticed a few guys from the neighborhood that were still there as well and finally saw Jamal's wife, Tiffany. They walked over to her. As soon as Tiffany saw Shawn, she burst into tears. Shawn hugged her.

"How is he?" Chanda asked.

Tiffany shook her head. "There are so many tubes going in and out of him and he's hooked up to so much. I want to hold him and let him know that I'm here and I love him but I'm afraid to touch him." She sniffed and wiped her eyes. "The doctors don't expect him to make it to the morning and right now, I'm just counting the minutes and begging God for another hour as they pass by."

"Is my mom here?" Shawn asked.

"She went to get some coffee for her and some tea for me. I can't believe this is happening," Tiffany said in tears.

Chanda hugged her and rubbed her back. "It's going to be okay. Jamal is a fighter. He loves you, he love's y'all son and he's going to fight to get through this. Trust me."

Tiffany nodded her head trying to stay strong. Shawn heard his wife's words of encouragement and he held onto them as he believed the same thing. But when he opened the door to Jamal's hospital room, all hope was dashed.

"Oh…" he mumbled. He froze where he was standing as he looked his older brother over and the very real possibility that Jamal could die hit him like a ton of bricks. He trembled as he stood there, unable to take any steps towards his brother to sit by him. He felt Chanda rub his back and jumped.

"Sit with him, Shawn. Tell him you're here." Chanda said softly as she sniffed back her tears.

Shawn managed to walk over to his brother and sat in a chair next to him but didn't know what to say. He listened to the machines and looked at all of them, using them as a distraction so he did not have to look at the bad shape his older brother was in.

A nurse came in and began checking his vitals. She glanced at Shawn not recognizing him at first and then did a double take.

"Oh my God! You're Shawn Williams that play for the Miami Heat! Oh my God! I'm such a huge fan of yours! I've seen all of your games and you are just so cool to watch. Oh my God! My brother is going to FA-LIP when I tell him I met you. Can you sign…" the young nurse caught herself when she saw the pain in Shawn's face. She glanced at Chanda who looked like she was two seconds away from smacking the shit out of her and then she looked at her patient chart, reading the name on it. "Jamal Williams…" she said softly. "I'm sorry… I'm so sorry. I didn't… You probably have all kinds of questions. I'll get the doctor for you…" she bumped into a table almost knocking some items over and then excused herself as she left the hospital room. Moments later, a doctor came in.

"Mr. Williams?" the doctor spoke, sounding more professional than the nurse that had been in the room moments before.

Yani

Shawn stood up and shook the doctor's hand when it was extended to him. "How's my brother?"

The doctor was quiet for a moment. "Your brother's injuries are extensive. A bullet pierced his lung. And there are still a few fragments that need to be removed. We're waiting for him to stabilize so we can go back in."

"How come you can't just do it now?" Shawn asked.

"Well, because if we go in before your brother is stable, so many things could go wrong. With his blood pressure being higher, he could stroke out. We also run the risk of him bleeding out. It's important that his blood continues to clot on its own which essentially is the key to his recovery."

"So he's going to make it, right?" Shawn asked with a hopeful look on his face.

The doctor sighed. "I'm going to be honest with you. He's in for a fight. A hell of a fight. It honestly doesn't look good, but we will do everything we can to save his life."

Shawn nodded his head as he fought back his tears. He sat back in the chair near Jamal and put his hands to his face. Chanda stood in front of him and he leaned his head against her stomach as he let out shoulder shaking sobs.

The same nurse came back in the room with a pen and pad looking as though she was about to ask Shawn for his autograph.

Chanda snapped. "If you don't get the fuck out of this room, I swear to God I'ma smack your boney ass through that fucking door! Get out!!" she screamed.

The nurse scrambled from the room and Chanda shook her head. They had been through so much growing up. She couldn't bear the thought of Shawn watching his only brother die. She continued to console him as she begged God for a small miracle.

15

Officer Curtis Daniels, who fired one of the first bullets as well as the bullet that hit Jamal in the back, lay in his bed sleeping peacefully, unaware of the pending demise waiting for him in his bedroom.

Andre walked over to his bed slowly as though he was stalking his prey. D-Ball stood on one side of the bed and Andre stood on the other. Andre pulled out a sawed off shot-gun and rubbed the barrel of it across Curtis' lips, waking him. The officer jumped, startled over seeing Andre and D-Ball in his room.

"Scream and I'll decorate this muthafucking room with your muthafucking head," Andre threatened in a cold voice as he cocked the shot gun.

Curtis looked at the both of them with wide eyes trembling, wondering what this could be about.

"Sit the fuck up and put your hands behind your back," D-Ball said. He had changed his clothes to a pair of black Dickie pants and a large Black hoody. He put on a black hat that pulled over his face like a mask with the face of a sinister looking skeleton. As many times as he joked around calling Andre "Death", that is exactly who he resembled that night.

Curtis sat up slowly watching the muzzle of the shot-gun as it moved in his direction. He glanced up at Andre who looked at him with cold, lifeless eyes before putting his hands behind his back like he was instructed to.

D-Ball handcuffed him and then wrapped duct tape around his wrists over the handcuffs. He came around the other side of the bed and wrapped his ankles with duct tape as well. Curtis was terrified and showed his fear through the warm stream of piss that eased down his legs. D-Ball snatched his glove covered hand back when he felt it.

"This scared little pussy sitting here pissing on himself," D-Ball grimaced.

"Oh you scared now, huh? You wasn't scared to shoot my son in the back, you fucking coward!" Andre hissed before hitting Curtis across the jaw with the butt of his gun. Blood flew from his mouth as he fell back onto the bed, hitting his head on the headboard.

D-Ball climbed on the bed and stuffed a gag in his mouth before placing a layer of duct tape around the back of his head to secure it. He then threw a cotton sack over his head and they dragged him from the bed. Curtis tried to plead for his life as they dragged him down the hallway and down his stairs, his head hitting every other step as they went down. They dragged him through the dining room and down into the basement before slinging him onto the floor.

Andre sat his shot-gun down and reached in his duffle bag, grabbing his silenced revolver. D-Ball stopped him.

"Not like that. I want it slow. I want him to feel his last fucking breath," D-Ball said as he began running water in the huge bath sink in the basement. He reached under the sink and grabbed a bucket, beginning to fill it up. "But first, I want some muthafucking answers."

Andre dragged Curtis across the floor near the drain and snatched the cotton sack from his head. His face and head was bruised from being hit with the butt of the shot-gun and then dragged down two flights of stairs. He looked up at them groggy, his vision blurry and suffering from a slight headache.

"Take the gag out of his mouth," D-Ball instructed. "Same shit still applies, you scream and my man right here will redecorate your basement with your fucking brains, bitch."

Andre chambered a round and squatted in front of Curtis with the same cold look in his eyes.

"Last night, you and some other cops shot another cop in front of 7-11 on Willow Grove Avenue. You niggas knew he was a cop so don't sit here and lie. What I want to know is, who ordered the hit on him?"

"I don't know what you're talking about," Curtis replied trembling.

"Wrong answer." D-Ball threw a towel over his face and began to pour the water over it. Curtis gagged and choked, moving his head to avoid the water, but D-Ball kept pouring. He sat the bucket back in the sink, adding more water to it. He then kicked Curtis in his back and in his ribs. Curtis coughed and gagged in between yelping like a dog each time D-Ball's foot connected with his body. "Who sent you, bitch?! Answer me!"

Andre stepped back feeling as though D-Ball didn't need his assistance. He pulled up a chair and took a seat.

After the fourth time of having massive amounts of water poured on his face and losing the strength to avoid it, feeling like he was drowning slowly, Curtis finally gave them the information that D-Ball requested, which only infuriated him more.

No longer wanting to pour water over Curtis' face he flung the bucket to the side. He plugged the sink up with the rubber stopper and ran ice cold water inside until it was filled almost to the top.

"Get 'cha bitch ass up," D-Ball sneered as he snatched Curtis by his collar. He was too weak to resist as D-Ball dragged him over to the sink.

"Please… I told you what you wanted to know. Please," Curtis begged. But his pleas for mercy fell on deaf ears. Andre watched D-Ball as he dunked Curtis' head into the sink filled with ice-cold water with Curtis putting up a struggle, but he was no match for the stronger D-Ball. Andre watched from where he was sitting, expecting D-Ball to let him up a few times and then dunk him back under. But D-Ball was serious about his business, and wanted that muthafucka dead.

"You dead yet, bitch?" D-Ball asked with sarcasm a moment after Curtis was no longer moving. He pulled Curtis from the water and looked at him. "Let me be sure." He dunked Curtis' head deep into the cold water for a few more minutes and then flung him onto the floor. He looked at him for a moment and then stepped over him as though he wasn't shit, walking over to Andre and taking the gun from him. He then turned and put two in Curtis' head. "Rather be safe than sorry." He handed Andre his gun back and began packing everything up without saying anything. He clipped the duct tape that was around Curtis' ankles and hands and removed the handcuffs as well. Andre watched him without saying a word, beginning to wonder if he had unleashed a monster. When D-Ball was sure that everything was cleaned up, he double checked the bedroom and then left.

Andre revved up the engine and drove off. D-Ball was quietly staring out of the window. He pulled his phone from his pocket and texted Tiffany. *"Any news???"* A few moments later, she texted back. *"Nothing yet. Shawn and Chanda are here. He's still critical."* D-Ball didn't bother responding. He tucked his phone back in his pocket.

"You alright over there, young-blood?" Andre asked as he continued to drive.

"Yeah, I'm straight," D-Ball replied in a low voice.

"What was that back there?"

D-Ball shrugged. "Killing them quick is too much of a favor. Jamal was in pain when they left him on the ground shot the fuck up and in handcuffs. He's in pain now. They should feel his pain," he said in a cold, flat voice.

Andre didn't say anything in return. If he wasn't sure before, he was positive now that he had indeed unleashed a monster with D-Ball and God help anyone who got in his way.

15

Cyndrell took a chance going into an all-night diner so he could charge his phone and get something warm to drink since he was wandering around with only his hoody on. He ordered a small coffee and a muffin and sat in the back near an outlet. He plugged his phone in and pulled his hood up over his head. A young waitress came over to him bringing his coffee and his muffin. She looked him over.

"You alright?" she asked him. Cyndrell nodded his head. "You look a little young to be out this time of night."

"I'm eighteen," Cyndrell lied.

"Oh okay. Well, my name is Gina. If you need anything else, just give me a holla." Cyndrell nodded his head again as he turned his cell phone on. He was bombarded with text messages from his mom and some of his other friends asking where he was. He even received a text from his English teacher suggesting he turn himself in rather than make things worse.

"Bitch, fuck outta here," he mumbled. He scrolled through some more of his texts and saw the one from Amora. He was feeling hopeless until he saw her message. *'I'm okay, Shorty. Get some sleep. I'll holla at you later."* He sat his phone down and picked over his muffin, not feeling very hungry. Instead, he sipped his coffee hoping that it would keep him awake. But before he knew it, he had nodded off to sleep.

Gina shook him and he popped awake, startled. He squinted, looking around and noticed it was daylight. "Hey, I didn't mean to scare you. You looked tired so I left you alone back here but, my shift is just about over and my manager will be here soon. He'll be pissed if he catches you sleeping in here and I don't want to get in trouble."

"It's cool. Thanks, yo." Cyndrell replied. He reached in his pocket and pulled out a couple of ones and handed them to her as a tip. "I know it's not much, but you looked out. Where I come from, you show love to people who look out for you."

Gina smiled. "Thanks." Cyndrell appeared cute to her and she was developing a curiosity about him. "Listen, my car is out front. Do you need a ride anywhere?"

Cyndrell was about to take her up on that offer when he noticed two cops come in and begin ordering their food. Gina noticed the scared expression on his face and turned to see what he was looking at. Cyndrell unplugged his phone and quietly got up.

"Um, do y'all have a bathroom in here?" he asked nervously.

"What, you on the run or something?" Gina joked quietly. Cyndrell didn't answer her and her eyes grew wide. "Oh my God, you are, aren't you?"

"Shorty, I ain't on the run because I did something. More like because I saw something I wasn't supposed to see," Cyndrell quickly explained. He checked the time on his phone and saw that it was almost 6:30 in the morning.

"There's a door that leads out to the alley way," Gina told him.

"Thanks, Shorty." Cyndrell said. He made his way over to the back door and left out, hurrying down the alley way as quickly as he could. He suddenly had an urge to urinate and went over to some bushes to relieve himself. When he was done, he exited the alley way and walked swiftly down the street. He tried to act casual, not wanting to look around too much and draw suspicion to himself. A cop car rolled by him and he hesitated, cursing under his breath.

"Fuck," he mumbled to himself. "Keep going, keep going, keep going," he said as he slowed his pace. The cop car drove a little further but then stopped and began to back up. Cyndrell knelt down as though he was tying his shoe, fighting the urge to run.

"Excuse me sir, did you see a Hispanic male run through here, about 5'9, medium build, wearing a Bellargo shirt and a pair of sweatpants?"

Cyndrell let out a sigh of relief. "Uh, yeah he just ran by me as I was coming out the house. I figured he was running for the bus," he lied.

"No, he just stuck a young woman up. Be careful out here," the cop warned him.

"Thank you, sir." Cyndrell replied. He waited for the cop to drive away before he got up. His phone went off making him jump. He saw that it was Amora and answered it. "Yo!"

"Hey. I was just checking on you to make sure you were okay," Amora said quietly in the phone as she peeked out of her bedroom.

"Yeah, I'm straight. I chilled in a diner until a little while ago. The waitress let me sleep for a little bit while I charged my phone. I turned it on and got all these texts from people asking why I was on the news and what was up. Fucking nut-ass Mrs. Knight gon' text me talking about some turn myself in to the authorities. Like bitch, please," Cyndrell spat.

Amora put her hand over her mouth to suppress her giggle. "Yeah, people been texting me too, asking if I know where you are." She hesitated for a moment. "Did you get my message?"

"Yeah, I got it. Did you mean it?"

"Yes," Amora said bashfully.

Cyndrell smiled. "One hundred, shorty. You going to school today?"

"No. My mom and dad are letting me stay home to keep the cops from trying anything slick like questioning me while they aren't around."

"Oh, alright. What time are they going to work? Can I come through?"

"They're about to leave, now," Amora told him.

"Alright, I'ma be there soon." Cyndrell disconnected the call and adjusted his hood on his head before he made his way over to Amora's house.

17

While Cyndrell was sleeping in the diner, D-Ball received a text from Sketch telling him that Nunez never left work. D-Ball double checked to make sure Sketch wasn't trying to pull a fast one on him and make off with the five grand that he gave to him. He patched into the online work schedule and saw that Nunez was scheduled to work a double. After what had been done to Jamal, he wanted to kill that bitch himself. He instructed Andre to drive to her house. Andre quickly put her address in his GPS and they drove over there. Shortly after they parked, Nunez was pulling up in front of her house. D-Ball quickly screwed the silencer on his gun and got out of the truck just as Nunez was putting the key in her door.

"Psst, Nunez." D-Ball whispered. Before she had a chance to turn around. D-Ball shot her twice in the back of her head. Thankfully, the blood didn't splatter on her front door. He pushed the door open slightly and then shoved her body inside as though he was stuffing junk in a closet. He twisted the lock on the door knob, tossed the keys in the house and closed the door behind him before he casually walked back to Andre's truck as though nothing happened.

"Holy shit, this nigga ain't playing," Andre mumbled to himself as he watched D-Ball walk back to the truck. He got inside without saying anything.

"You hungry?" D-Ball asked Andre without looking at him.

"Naw, I'm good young-blood." Andre said quietly. He peered at D-Ball out the corner of his eye as he drove down the street. The silence in the truck was a bit unnerving so he turned the radio on. *Monster* by Eminem and Rhianna was playing. Andre burst out laughing. "How fitting…"

D-Ball disregarded his comment and remained quiet as he plotted on his next target.

18

Amora pretended to be asleep when her parents were getting ready to leave for work. She listened out for her father's car to leave out of their driveway and when she was sure they were gone, she jumped from her bed and ran in the bathroom to get cleaned up. Just as she was finishing brushing her teeth, her phone went off with a text from Cyndrell letting her know that he was in her backyard. Butterflies filled her stomach as she hurried down the stairs and to the back door to open it for him.

"What's up?" Cyndrell spoke as he gave her a hug. Amora let him in and closed the door behind him.

"Nothing. People still texting me but at this point, I'm not even responding. They're just being nosey." Amora told him.

"I know, right?" Cyndrell agreed as he sat at the counter in her kitchen. He looked exhausted. "I don't mean to drawl Shorty, but can I take a shower. I feel like a dirty-ass young bol still wearing the same shit from yesterday, been walking the streets and shit. I smell like North Philly out this bitch," he half-way joked.

Amora chuckled. "Yeah, we got a bathroom with a shower downstairs. I'll throw your stuff in the washing machine and give you one of my dad's shirt and sweatpants to put on while you wait," she told him as she went over to the basement. Cyndrell followed behind her.

There were towels and wash cloths folded up on a table in the basement. She passed him one of each and left out the bathroom as he got undressed.

While he was in the shower, she ran up to her parents' room and grabbed the shirt and sweatpants for Cyndrell to put on. She didn't want to barge in the bathroom while he was showering, so Amora decided to put his things in the washing machine while she waited.

"Amora, come here." Cyndrell called to her. She grabbed the things she had for him and took them in the bathroom. It was hot and steamy, and though she couldn't see too much, she glimpsed enough of his body to almost make her lose her breath. They had never seen each other naked before, and outside of some heavy make-out sessions, they had not been sexually active with each other either. Amora was a virgin but assumed Cyndrell had experience. Little did she know, he was a virgin as well.

He noticed the way she avoided looking at him by staring at the floor and didn't say anything as he dried off. He took the sweatpants from her and began putting them on as Amora continued to look everywhere else except at him. It was something about her shy behavior that was a turn on for him so he walked over to her.

"Oh my God," Amora thought to herself.

Cyndrell grabbed her hand and placed it on his abs. He had taken an interest in boxing and was heavily into working out so for a 16-year-old, his body was amazing. Amora explored his tight abs with the tips of her fingers tracing over them like a child discovering a new toy. Cyndrell ran his fingers through her hair and kissed her. They stood in the bathroom making out as the steam seeped out of the room. Cyndrell began backing her out of the bathroom and over to the sofa before laying her down on it. His hands began exploring her body as well while he kissed her neck. He traced his tongue over her chin and kissed her again.

"Cyndrell…I'm… I'm a virgin." Amora said innocently.

Cyndrell looked at her with a grin. "Good. So am I."

Yani

Amora looked at him shocked. *"Yes!"* she thought to herself.

"We don't have to do anything, Shorty. If you don't want to, I can wait." Cyndrell told her.

Amora shook her head quickly. "No, I want to." She sat up from under him and unsnapped her bra before Cyndrell helped her out of her shirt. Though her body was flawless with smooth caramel skin and no scars, she placed her hands over her chest hiding herself from him.

Cyndrell took his sweatpants back off and then took hers off also before laying back on the couch with her. They continued their make-out session, feeling over each other. Amora wanted more. She fought with herself to build up the courage to touch his manhood, letting him know that she was ready and wanted it. Cyndrell felt how moist she was and tried to enter her, not thinking to use a condom and Amora didn't stop him. Her nails scraped his back as she felt him entering her and she gritted her teeth against the pain. She gasped when she felt him slip inside of her and a tear slid out of the corner of her eye.

"I can stop," Cyndrell said in a breathy tone, praying she didn't tell him to. Her tight wetness was driving him crazy.

Amora shook her head. "No, don't stop."

Cyndrell positioned himself on top of her and kissed her again as he pushed himself deeper inside of her. He moved slow as though he was dancing with her to the sounds of her soft moans. But the scratching of his back, the wetness between her legs and the way her tongue danced around his mouth was driving him crazy. He went harder and deeper causing Amora to moan louder until her body began to shake under his. She clung to him as she climaxed and not meaning to, he came inside of her, hard and deep. Amora wrapped her legs around him, still trembling and breathing heavy. Cyndrell watched her as she stared up at the ceiling trying to catch her breath.

"Do you still love me, Shorty?" he asked her quietly.

Amora looked at him and nodded her head. "Yes."

Cyndrell nodded his head also and then laid on her chest. He intertwined his fingers with hers and before they knew it, they both fell asleep.

Yani

19

"Charge to 250!" a doctor yelled. "Clear!" the paddles sent currents through Jamal's body causing him to jerk. They paused a moment to see if anything changed but the monitors still hummed the flat lining tune. Tiffany could be heard screaming from the back of the hospital room, begging the doctors to save him and begging Jamal to keep fighting.

"Get her out of here!" the doctor yelled. Tiffany struggled with the nurses who tried to usher her out of the room. Shawn grabbed her and picked her up before taking her out to the hall. He held her tightly, muffling her cries and her screams as Chanda, Deisha, Maurice and his mother stood to the side trying to remain strong.

Tiffany was muttering something as she sobbed in Shawn's arms. He swallowed back his own tears as he watched the door, barely breathing while praying that Jamal wasn't dead. It seemed like forever before one of the doctors came out of the room.

"We got him back. It was a close one, but we got him back. If we can get him stable in the next hour, then we can go back in and try to get the fragments out and repair the rest of the damage the bullets left behind. But I have to tell you, as much as it pains me to say this, you may want to prepare yourselves… you may want to gather the rest of his family up here to say their good-byes." And with those words, the doctor went back into Jamal's room with the rest of the doctors so they could finish assessing him and discuss what the next steps should be.

Keyona plopped in a chair and burst into tears. Chanda put her arm around her and held her as her own tears flowed. None of them knew what to say as they all hung onto the doctor's last statement advising them to prepare themselves.

Shawn reached in his pocket and pulled his cellphone so he could call his father. It went straight to voicemail. "Dad," he said into the phone. "I don't know what you're doing or where you are, but you need to get back to the hospital. Jamal is…" he hesitated for a moment and then his grief broke through all the strength he was trying to display since he made it to Philly. "Jamal is dying," he said in tears. "Mom needs you… I need you." He disconnected the call and stuck his phone back in his pocket.

Yani

***

Tiffany sat in the passenger seat of Jamal's Infiniti blind-folded. "Where are we going?" she asked.

"Patience, babe." Jamal said as he parked the car. He got out and opened her door before helping her from the car. She was five months pregnant and glowed with her plump, round stomach. Jamal held her hands and pulled her towards him as he backed up the walk-way to a house and then stopped her. He then stood behind her and wrapped his arms around her waist before kissing the side of her mouth.

"Can I take the blind fold off, now?" she asked with a smile.

"Take it off," he told her.

Tiffany reached up to the blind fold and pulled it down so it hung around her neck. She opened her mouth and gasped.

"Welcome home," Jamal said in her ear.

"Stop playing, Jamal!" Tiffany squealed as she looked at the front of the house. They had driven by it for the last two months and each time they drove past it, she expressed how much she would love to buy that house and have it for when the baby was born. "Are you serious?"

"I'm dead ass serious. There's nothing I wouldn't do for you and there's nothing I wouldn't give you. I love you, Tiff. I love you with everything I have inside of me."

"Damn, boy you about to make me cry." Tiffany gushed. She turned her head so she could kiss Jamal. "I love you too, babe."

Jamal began walking her to the front door and unlocked it. When he opened the door, Tiffany's jaw damn near hit the floor. The house was immaculate. There were shiny, golden hardwood floors and cream colored walls. The bulb ceiling lights lit up the living room like a brightly lit stage awaiting its performer. The dining room was huge with a crystal chandelier hanging from the ceiling and the kitchen was complete with marble granite counter tops, an island and all stainless steel appliances. Tiffany squealed when she saw the six eye stove with a side grill and large oven as well as the double-door stainless steel refrigerator. The big bay window would let in lots of sunlight and over-looked a large backyard that already had her plotting on the vegetables and flowers she was going to plant back there. She noticed that Jamal wasn't looking in the kitchen with her after she'd finished checking out the appliances. When she went back into the living room and was about to call out his name, she noticed the rose pedals making a trail that led up the steps. She held onto the banister and followed the rose pedals. She saw where they led to the front bedroom but stopped briefly to take a peek at what the bathroom looked like. Tiffany almost died when she saw the large Jacuzzi bath tub. She looked ahead at the front bedroom and noticed there was a light flickering so she made her way down the hall and pushed the bedroom door open. She looked around with her mouth hanging open. Jamal had candles lit around the room and the trail of rose pedals stopped on the floor in the shape of a heart. In the center was a black ring box.

"Jamal…" Tiffany said breathlessly as she stared at the box knowing what it was.

Jamal took her by the hand and walked her over to the heart-shaped rose pedals. He picked the ring box up and stood in front of her.

"I had this whole romantic speech thing that I was going to say and I can't remember none of that shit right now." Jamal laughed and Tiffany chuckled with him as her eyes became teary. "I came across a lot of women after Tamera who wanted to see me doing better. But you were the first and only one since her that made me better. You complete me, Tiff. You make me whole. I'm a better man with you. I'm a better man because of you. Every day I wake up, I want you to be the first person I see. Every night I go to sleep, I want you to be the last person I see, for the rest of my life. If you can stand me forever, can I have you forever?"

Tiffany was too choked up to form any words and put her hand to her mouth as she nodded her head yes to him.

"I need that hand," Jamal laughed as he pulled it away from her face. Her hand trembled as he slid the ring on her finger before he kissed her, long and deep.

"I love you, Jamal." Tiffany sniffed as she wrapped her arms around him.

"I love you, too…"

***

Tiffany sat at Jamal's bedside holding his hand. "If you can stand me forever, can I have you forever?" she said to him in a trembling voice. "Our forever is just beginning, Jamal. Please don't leave me… please." She sniffed and squeezed his hand as she continued to bargain with God to spare her husband. When she looked at him, she noticed a tear slide from his eye and she began to fear that forever wasn't going to be as long as she hoped it would be.

20

The news of Sheila Armstrong's murder along with Nunez and Curtis Daniels was on the news 24/7. They were being headlined as an attack on police. What the public saw as an all-out man-hunt was nothing more than a facade. The police knew they wouldn't be able to explain why they were searching for Dante Smith and Andre Williams without giving into the rumors that Jamal's shooting was more than what they were alluding to, considering his car had just blown up a couple of days before and he along with his wife and father were ambushed at his home that same night. So, Jamal's shooting was said to be an isolated event and a possible case of mistaken identity. And even though most of the cops knew that the three killings were in retaliation for what was done to Jamal, they refused to speculate or put that idea in the media's head.

Andre had been given a heads up by Felix and George that the police were beefing up their security and were positive that Dante was involved in the killings even though there were no witnesses and no camera footage anywhere that could link him to the killings. They weren't one hundred percent sure that Andre was involved, but they knew Dante was getting help from somewhere.

Andre tried to suggest to D-Ball that he sit tight for a little bit instead of bringing so much heat to himself. But at that present moment in time, D-Ball was in a very dark place and felt like he had nothing else to lose after what was done to Jamal.

"Why are you backing out of catching these muthafuckas?" D-Ball asked Andre as they were sitting in his truck getting something to eat. "Weren't you the one who said you wouldn't rest until you laid them all down six feet deep even if that meant you had to be laid right behind them?"

"I know what I said," Andre replied coldly.

"So what is the fucking problem?" D-Ball asked.

"The problem as I see it is you're running around here like the muthafucking terminator like you're untouchable. Everybody can be touched, one way or another. I just think we need to find this kid and make sure we get to him before the cops do. I'm all for dishing out some head shots. But what good is that if the evidence we need gets into the wrong hands and my boy's shooting goes down as some bullshit where all the cops get off with a slap on the wrist," Andre replied.

"Fine, fuck it. Let's do it your way. Where did George say the kid was last?" D-Ball replied as he stuffed some French fries into his mouth.

"He's been with the girlfriend all morning. George just text the address." Andre replied as he started the truck.

"Alright, let's go get this kid."

They drove over to Amora's house. Since she was home from school, her parents didn't bother putting the alarm on. Not wanting to raise any suspicions among neighbors who may have been home peeping out of their windows, D-Ball and Andre went around back. D-Ball picked the lock effortlessly and shook his head.

"When will niggas learn that just because you move from the hood doesn't mean you're untouchable?" he mumbled. They slipped inside silently and found Amora and Cyndrell asleep on the couch. Andre placed his finger to his ear when he heard George say something in his Bluetooth.

"Cops are fifteen minutes away. You guys gotta hurry."

"How the fuck…?" D-Ball grimaced as he looked around.

"The same way I found him. His GPS is on." George explained.

Andre walked over to the two of them and nudged them. Amora woke up first and was about to scream but Andre put his hand over her mouth. Cyndrell felt her move and woke up also. He jumped when he saw the gun.

"She didn't have anything to do with it, bruh. Just take me." Cyndrell said trying to be brave. Andre smirked.

"Chill out, young blood. We ain't 5-0. But you might wanna move like your ass depends on it because they're on their way here now." Andre told him. "Put some clothes on."

Dante peeped out of the window growing impatient, quickly. He didn't want to run the risk of having a shoot-out while there were kids around.

Andre turned his back while Amora and Cyndrell got dressed.

"How do I know you're not one-time?" Cyndrell asked as he threw his hoody on.

"I'm not. But he is," Andre said as he nodded at D-Ball. Cyndrell looked at him.

D-Ball turned to face him. "You recorded my partner getting shot last night. I'm not here as a cop. I'm here to make sure the cops don't smoke your ass on some "we feared for our lives" type shit, so they can take what you recorded and destroy it without anyone else knowing about it.

"Guys, you gotta move, fast. They are five minutes and closing." George warned them.

"Shit!" D-Ball said as he pulled both of his guns. He waved Amora and Cyndrell towards the door.

"I can't leave! What about my parents?" Amora panicked.

"Your parents will be cashing in a life insurance policy if you don't move your ass. These guys don't leave witnesses." D-Ball said to her. Cyndrell grabbed her by the arm and they hurried out of the house, but they were too late.

There were only two cop cars that pulled up. D-Ball stood with his hands behind his back as he watched them. He was ready for war.

One of the cops got out of the car not recognizing D-Ball. "Cyndrell Matthews, you're wanted for questioning in last night's shooting on Willow Grove Avenue. We need you to come with us."

"Nah, he ain't going nowhere with y'all." D-Ball said as he looked at the four cops.

Another cop looked at D-Ball and recognized him. He pulled his gun but was too slow. Andre already had his gun drawn and caught him twice in the stomach. Cyndrell and Amora ducked for cover as gun fire erupted between Andre and D-Ball and the other officers.

"Run! Now!" Andre yelled to Cyndrell and Amora.

Cyndrell grabbed Amora's hand and they took off running. D-Ball took out two of the police officers and Andre took out a third. He jumped in the driver side of the truck and D-Ball jumped in the passenger seat. He quickly began to reload his gun. Instead of the last cop shooting at Andre and D-Ball, he aimed his gun at Cyndrell and fired. The bullet hit Cyndrell in his upper back near his right shoulder. He hollered out before falling forward on the ground.

It seemed like everything moved in slow motion for Amora at that moment. She turned around facing the direction the gunshot came from, horrified. The cop turned his gun on her and was set to pull his trigger but D-Ball beat him to it, firing a bullet into his head.

Andre whipped his truck around and sped over to where Cyndrell and Amora were. His truck came to a screeching halt.

Amora was crying hysterically, shaking Cyndrell and calling for him to get up but he wasn't moving.

D-Ball checked him and then Andre helped him get Cyndrell in the back of the truck.

"Amora!" D-Ball yelled. "Get his phone and get in the fucking truck! More cops will be here soon, we gotta move!"

Yani

Amora snatched his phone from the ground and jumped in the back of the truck as Andre sped off.

"He's not moving! He's not moving!" Amora cried.

"Put your hands where he's bleeding and hold pressure. He's still alive. If we can get him to the hospital, he'll make it. Just keep pressure on it. And for God's sake, shut that fucking screaming up in my ear!" D-Ball shouted.

"That was not supposed to go down like that. Not like that. Fuck! You know what type of shit storm we're in right now?" Andre said angrily as he drove quickly to Abington Memorial Hospital.

"We can't fucking worry about that right now man, just drive and get this kid to the hospital." D-Ball said in return.

They pulled up to the hospital and carefully took Cyndrell out before hurrying inside of the emergency room. Doctors came on the run and began assisting him. They put him on a gurney and wheeled him into an exam room, closing the door in Amora's face.

"Do you have his phone?" D-Ball asked her.

Amora trembled as she looked at the blood on her hands and on her clothes. Her body shook as she tried to process what just happened. Just a few hours ago they were making love and everything was perfect. And now her boyfriend was laying on a gurney shot, and possibly dying. D-Ball grabbed her and spun her around.

"Listen, I know what just happened was scary. But what's even more scary is getting the death penalty for killing a cop or going to jail for life for being an accessory to a cop's murder. So with that being said, do you have his phone?"

Amora nodded her head and reached in her back pocket. She pulled it out and gave it to D-Ball. Andre walked over to him.

"Fuck, the muthafucker is locked." D-Ball said angrily. "Do you know his password?" he asked Amora.

Amora shook her head, still too shook up to form her words.

Andre called George. "George, I need you to crack this phone. He has a password on it and the girlfriend doesn't know it."

"Okay, bring it to me. I can unlock it in no time. What is it, an iPhone?" George asked.

"Yeah," Andre replied.

"Yeah, I got you. Just bring it."

D-Ball looked at Amora. "The cops will be here soon. Don't say anything. Don't answer any questions. They're going to try to intimidate you and threaten you and scare you with all kinds of bullshit. Do you love Cyndrell?"

Amora nodded her head as the tears came again.

"Good. Then for the sake of his life, his freedom, your life, your freedom, don't fucking fold. The only thing you say is I want my phone call. Understand?"

Amora nodded her head.

"You did good today, Shorty." And with those words, D-Ball hurried behind Andre and they got in his truck and hurried to George and Felix, knowing they were running out of time.

21

Tiffany was lying across the bed propped up on some pillows. She had reached the full term mark in her pregnancy and was expecting their son to arrive any day. Jamal rubbed her feet while they talked and watched Kevin Hart's stand-up comedy, *Laugh at My Pain*.

"Lord, that feels so good," Tiffany said in a tired voice. She leaned her head back on the pillow and closed her eyes as Jamal rubbed her foot.

"Little Man act like he don't wanna come outta there," Jamal said to her with a smile.

Tiffany shook her head. "I swear to God, man if he don't bust a move by Friday, I'm evicting his ass that night." Jamal burst out laughing. "You laughing and I'm dead ass serious. He got to go. My back hurts, my feet are swollen. I look a mess."

"You look beautiful girl, chill out." Jamal said to her.

Tiffany rolled her eyes. "Whatever. You know you're tired of sleeping on the edge of the bed because my big ass taking up all the space."

Jamal leaned over to her and gave her a kiss on the cheek. "It's not that deep, Tiff."

"Yeah? And neither is the depth of my bladder anymore. That's something I won't miss, the constant trips to the bathroom. I swear I think whenever I get comfortable, this boy starts tap dancing on my bladder." Jamal chuckled again as he helped her up from the bed. She waddled a little and then stopped, feeling an uncomfortable cramping feeling. She took a deep breath and waited a moment before trying to go to the bathroom again. She made it about half way down the hall when she really felt the urge to go and tried to move a little faster.

SPLASH!

"Oooooh…" Tiffany said as she looked down. She felt another gush even though she tried to hold it. "Oooh! OOOOH! JAMAL!!!" She screamed.

"Yeah, babe." Jamal called back to her as he came to the bedroom doorway.

Tiffany cringed when she felt tiny squirts leaking out of her. "I think my water just broke."

Jamal looked at the way she was standing as though she had just wet herself and then ran down the hall to her. "You sure you didn't just piss yourself?" Jamal teased.

Tiffany sneered at him. "You better be glad my leg can't reach otherwise I'd kick you in the got-damn neck!"

"You violent as shit," Jamal chuckled. "Stay right here." He ran to the room and grabbed the baby bag that was in the closet as well as a dry pair of sweatpants. When he got back to her, she was leaning into the wall, holding her stomach.

Tiffany winced before squealing. "Shit, I wasn't expecting this to hurt from the gate like this." Jamal helped her out of the wet pants she had on and put the other sweats on her before getting her to the car. The contractions were coming hella fast and Tiffany couldn't help but to cry.

They got to a red light and a contraction came full force. She slammed her fist against the car door. "Why every time we get to a fucking red light, a fucking contraction comes?" she grimaced. "Mannn, jump this shit!" she yelled at Jamal.

"You're trying to get me a ticket, Tiff." Jamal said in a surprisingly calm voice.

Tiffany snatched him by his collar. "You're a fucking cop! Jump the fucking light!" she screamed.

Jamal stepped on the gas after making sure no cars were coming and hurried up and got her to the hospital. The last thing he wanted her to do was beat his ass in the car.

"Ugh! I wanna push!" Tiffany whined as the nurses were wheeling her to labor and delivery.

"No Ms. Fields! Whatever you do, don't push!" the nurses told her.

Less than three hours later, Tiffany was washed in sweat, trembling from the fierce labor pains and smiling as Jamal was holding their son-

Yani

Jamir Khaleem Williams. He leaned onto her bed as he held their son and the nurse was kind enough to take their picture as he was kissing her.

"You did good, babe. You did good." Jamal told her. Tiffany closed her tired eyes and rested her head against his, loving the baby sounds their newborn son was making.

***

The doctors came back in the room to check on Jamal and began talking amongst each other in a hushed tone. Tiffany watched them, trying to hear what they were saying and quickly became annoyed that they were acting so secretive.

"Please don't do that," she said to them. They turned and looked at her. "Whatever it is, I'm sure it's not that hard for me to follow."

The main doctor cleared his throat and put his hands behind his back. "We were hoping to get his pressure a little lower so there would be a higher chance of him coming out of the next surgery. The universal blood pressure for an adult is 120 over 80. Right now, Jamal is 132 over 86. He's been holding steady at that rate for the last couple of hours. We would like to go back in and try to repair as much of the damage as we can in hopes that he's strong enough to continue healing with the medications. But that's only if we have the family's permission."

Tiffany looked at them all for a space of heartbeats and then stood up. "Could you excuse me for just one second?" She walked over to the door and motioned Shawn and Keyona to come into the room. She asked the doctor to explain it again. After he had done so, the room fell silent.

"If you need time to decide, we can come back. But it would be best if we did this sooner than later," the doctor said to them.

Tiffany looked at Keyona and Shawn. "What do you two think? Should they do the surgery now or try to wait until his blood pressure goes down a little lower?" she asked them.

"What happens if we wait any longer?" Shawn asked.

"We run the risk of infections and that would be one more battle his body has to fight. He could code on us again and we may or may not be able to bring him back around. The medicine and efforts used to stabilize him are really a waste if this operation is not done as soon as possible."

"Tiffany, you're his wife. You really should decide." Keyona told her.

Tiffany thought to herself. *"Great. If I okay the surgery, and he dies, they'll be on my ass about how I was too hasty and I should have waited. If I tell them to wait and he dies, they'll be on my ass about how I shouldn't have waited!"* She put her hands to her face, too exhausted and heartbroken to cry. She looked at Jamal wondering what he would tell her to do.

After a moment she looked at the doctors. "Do the surgery," she said firmly. The doctors nodded at her and left the room to prep the operating room.

"Tiff, you really need to get some sleep. You've been up for more than 24 hours," Keyona said to her. "That can't be good for you or the baby."

"I'm okay. Could you get me some more tea, please? And some crackers?" Tiffany asked as she slowly paced the room.

Keyona left the room and Shawn looked at her.

"You're pregnant again?" he asked her.

Tiffany nodded her head. "I had just told him before he left the house…" Tiffany shook her head, feeling dizzy. Shawn grabbed her and moved her to a chair.

"When's the last time you ate?" he asked her.

Tiffany thought for a moment. "Around six something last night. I nibbled on some crackers earlier and drank some tea. I'm okay," she insisted even though her body felt weak.

"You're not okay. Sit here and relax. I'll go get you some real food, alright?" Shawn told her.

Tiffany nodded her head and he left the room. She felt fatigue and weak, so she rested her head on her hands as she leaned on her knees. She needed Jamal to make it through this. She didn't want to live in a world without him.

Yani

22

D-Ball and Andre walked into the new safe house that George and Felix were held up in. They were watching the news coverage on the cops D-Ball and Andre had taken out. They were shocked that Andre's and D-Ball's pictures weren't plastered all over the television and couldn't understand why they weren't either. Instead, it was being reported that they responded to a robbery in the back of the houses and were ambushed by unknown assailants. Felix had a bad feeling that Andre and D-Ball's names were being kept hush because something else was being planned. He just wasn't sure what it was.

It didn't take long for George to unlock Cyndrell's phone. He plugged it in so it could charge before they checked out the video he had of Jamal's shooting. Once the phone was charged to a fair percentage, George sent the file to his computer and then pulled the video up on one of the screens. They watched in silence as everything unfolded. George's mouth hung open in disbelief. Felix turned away after Jamal was shot the first time. Andre's face was expressionless while D-Ball's held a look of rage.

"Turn it off," D-Ball told George when it got to the part where he arrived. "Turn the fucking video off."

George fumbled around for a moment and then stopped the video.

"We have the video. Now what?" D-Ball asked as he paced back and forth.

"We could upload it again. This time try putting it on YouTube." George suggested.

Andre shook his head. "Nah, they'll just take it down again."

"The media is dying to know why there is a "war" being waged against the police. How about we give them an exclusive. Let them know Jamal's shooting wasn't just a case of mistaken identity, but it was a hit. Then we can leak some of the documents that we have about what's going on in the department, and watch it burn down from there." Felix suggested.

"I was actually hoping to body a couple more niggas but…" D-Ball started to say but his phone went off. It was a video message from his girlfriend Nicole. He started not to open it wondering why she would be sending him a video message knowing that he was working at the time being. Something told him not to wait, and to open the video right at that moment. He froze as he watched what was sent. Three men had Nicole in their apartment The video was shaky, but D-Ball could see where she had been slapped around from the bruises around the corner of her mouth. She screamed as they tore her clothes off, yanking her around by her hair. The guys in the video had their faces covered with the same masks that D-Ball wore when he killed Officer Daniels. The fear in Nicole's eyes as they held her by her hair with a knife to her throat made D-Ball's blood boil. There was no verbal threat or ultimatum. One guy began to undo his belt and then the video went black.

D-Ball grabbed his gun and went over to the door. Andre ran to stop him.

"What are you doing?" Andre asked him as he grabbed his arm.

"They got my fucking girl. What the fuck do you mean what am I doing?" D-Ball grimaced as he looked at Andre as though he were stupid.

"It's a set-up, D-Ball! Use your head! They didn't make any threats, give any warnings, not to mention they were wearing the same fucking mask you wore when you offed Daniels.

Think about it. They want you to come there all hot-headed, and not thinking clearly so they can catch you slipping and take you out," Andre said to him firmly.

"So what the fuck am I supposed to do? Just let them rape and kill her?" D-Ball asked back. Andre didn't say anything. D-Ball stared at him for a moment and then looked at Felix and George. Felix shook his head while George looked at the floor and then D-Ball got it as though something clicked. More than likely Nicole was already dead or would be by the time he got there. His heart sank into his stomach as that thought passed. He had been with Nicole for a year and a half after Elizabeth left him claiming she couldn't handle the guns and the violence. He had fallen in love with her and couldn't take the idea that she was another casualty in everything that was going on. He then looked at George with fire in his eyes before storming over to him and snatching him by his collar. Felix jumped from his chair and tried to pry his hands off of him.

"Dante, what the hell are you doing?" Felix yelled.

"You said the cameras in the area were blacked out when we went to Daniel's crib."

"They were!" George squealed as he trembled in fear.

"Yeah? So explain to me why the fuck those muthafuckas were wearing the same got damn mask I wore when I took his ass out. How, bitch!?" D-Ball said as he shook the young hacker.

"I don't know…" George squealed some more.

Andre was able to pull D-Ball off George and separated the two.

D-Ball yanked away. "Fuck off me!"

Andre didn't back down. While he liked D-Ball and didn't want to have to hurt him, he wasn't beneath knocking his ass back in line seeing as though he was getting out of control.

D-Ball turned his back on them and squatted down with his hands to his head. He tried hard to hold back his anguish but the images of Jamal getting shot and lying on the ground handcuffed and bleeding as well as the kid Cyndrell and now his girlfriend, was too much to deal with in just one day. They watched not knowing what to say as D-Ball broke down in tears.

Andre knew it was coming. He understood how close D-Ball was with Jamal and knew that no matter how many people he killed to avenge his best friend's shooting, it wouldn't ease the pain or numb it. He placed his hand on D-Ball's shoulder and squeezed sympathetically to let him know that he was there.

"It's no point in uploading the video on line. We need to get this video out on a national level. And it needs to be at a time when a lot of people are watching the news." Felix suggested after it began to sound like D-Ball was calming down.

"The 5 o'clock news," George added.

"Exactly." Felix said in return. "Which only gives us about 45 minutes."

"Do it," Andre told them.

George jumped back into his chair and began typing. "NBC 10's got my vote. What about you guys?"

The other's agreed and George was able to mask one of his many Google voice numbers and texted a new reporter that was going to be on air at 5.

"That shooting on Willow Grove Avenue wasn't a case of mistaken identity. It was a hit on Detective Jamal Williams by the Philadelphia Police Department to neutralize him after the massive arrests and convictions he achieved three years ago. I have a video of the shooting as well as a witness. I'll give you and only you the video to air as a breaking news story." George sent in his message. Not even a minute later, the reporter was messaging him back.

"Who is this? And how do I know this video is legit?" the reporter asked back.

Yani

"It's legit. Do you want to be the one to break this story and be the first one with this footage or should I hand this over to Fox News?" George waited a minute before another message came in.

"Send it," the reporter told him.

"We got a gofer," George smiled. He attached the video to the reporter's private email.

"Now what?" D-Ball asked after he had gotten himself together.

"We turn on the news and we wait." Felix replied.

D-Ball leaned into the wall but couldn't stop thinking about his girlfriend Nicole. "I can't leave her there like that," he said as he shook his head.

Andre looked at him. "What do you mean?"

"Nicole, I can't just leave her there like that after seeing that video. I hear what you're saying, but I can't leave her like that. And if it was Keyona, or Shawn or Jamal and you got a video like the one I just got, you wouldn't leave them there either. You don't have to come with me. Whatever happens, happens. But I can't leave her there."

Andre stared at D-Ball for a second and then sighed, giving in. "Call your goons and tell them to meet us at the apartment so that we have back-up. How many can you get up there?"

"I got an army," D-Ball replied as he put his phone to his ear. "Sketch, I got some heat and I think my girl might have been caught in the cross fire. Round my niggas up and meet me at my crib ASAP. Anybody there that's not supposed to be there, smoke they fucking ass, you hear me?"

"100, yo!" Sketch replied. He disconnected the call and sent the word to some other guys. They hopped in their cars and made their way to D-Ball's apartment.

"The reporter just showed the video to her superiors to authenticate it. It's a go!" George said to the others in an excited tone.

"I need to get to my crib, Dre." D-Ball said to Andre.

Andre nodded his head. "Keep us updated if anything happens. We'll be back." Andre and D-Ball left to head back to his apartment.

D-Ball texted Nicole just to see if she would answer. Andre noticed from the corner of his eye that D-Ball kept checking his phone every few seconds. He felt bad for him and began to debate whether or not it would be a good idea for him to drive over to their apartment.

They pulled up in front of his complex and D-Ball immediately saw cars that most of his goons from North Philly were occupying. He jumped out the car and the guys got out, greeting him with handshakes and pounds.

"How's 'Mal?" Sketch asked. "We were going to go up there to check on him but we figured his family wanted some privacy."

"He holding his own. You know that nigga a beast. He's like Pac- five shots couldn't stop 'em, he took it and smiled," D-Ball said with a light chuckle, trying to make light of the situation."

"Good, that's my old-head yo. He's been looking out for me since these little kids tried to roll on me when he was coming home after Shawn got shot back summer of 2001," Sketch said as he rubbed his hands together. "So what's the move?"

"I just want a few of y'all to come with me. The rest of y'all stay out here just in case some shit pops off," D-Ball said. He signaled for Sketch and three other guys along with Andre to come with him.

They went inside of the building casually so they didn't alert any of the other tenants as they made their way up to his and Nicole's apartment. D-Ball's heart was pounding as he made his way down the hallway. He already had his gun drawn but partially hidden under his hooded sweat-shirt. When he got to the door of their apartment, he could feel it in the air that something wasn't right. The first red flag was the door wasn't closed all of the way. He pulled his gun and signaled for Andre and Sketch to cover him. They listened to see if they heard any movement in the apartment. After what felt like an eternity, D-Ball was sure that it was quiet, too quiet. He pushed the door open slowly and Andre and Sketch followed him in. The other guys remained outside to keep watch.

"Nicole!" D-Ball called out as he opened the bedroom door. The room was a mess. He could tell that a struggle went down by the way things were scattered onto the floor from the dresser. The mirror above the dresser was smashed as though someone had been slammed into it. Though it was the tail end of Fall and Winter was a few weeks away, the ceiling fan oscillated slowly above him. Sketch checked the living room and the kitchen but Andre stopped by the bathroom door. It was almost as though he could sense that something was deathly wrong in there. He pushed the bathroom door opened slowly and then closed his eyes before shaking his head.

"Dante…" he said. "In here."

D-Ball came from their bedroom and pushed his way into the bathroom before stopping in his tracks. Nicole lay on the floor by the tub, on her side with a black silk scarf around her neck where she had been raped, beaten and strangled to death. The mask, similar to the one D-Ball wore when he killed Officer Daniels, had been placed over her face. D-Ball knelt beside her unable to contain his grief. Even though the better part of him suspected before he got there that she had been killed, he's hoped that he was wrong. He pulled her into his arms and cradled her, sobbing loudly. Sketch hurried over to the bathroom when he heard D-Ball's cries. He put his hands to his head, sorry that D-Ball had taken that kind of loss.

Andre knelt beside him. "Dante, calls have to be made so they can move her."

D-Ball closed his eyes unable to think. The rage washed over his body and all he felt was an indescribable pain. First Jamal and now the woman he loved. Somebody was going to pay. Somebody was going to pay dearly.

Andre figured Dante was in no position to make any calls so he pulled his phone and made them for him. After he hung up, Felix called him. He stepped outside.

"Yeah?" Andre answered.

"Is anybody at the hospital with Tiffany and the rest of Jamal's family?" Felix asked.

"No, we just found Dante's girlfriend dead in their bathroom. Those muthafuckas beat her something fierce and then strangled her."

"Shit… that's not good." Felix replied as he shook his head.

"You fucking right it ain't. What happened to Jamal put him at the edge. This might send him over it."

Felix shook his head. "Well, George just got word that NBC 10 is going to air Jamal's shooting at 6 o'clock as their breaking news story and they are airing it unedited. Somebody needs to be at the hospital with Tiffany and his mom and brother to make sure they don't see this."

"Say no more. I'm on my way." Andre disconnected the call and went back to D-Ball.

"I gotta head to the hospital. Will you be alright here?" Andre asked him. D-Ball only nodded his head. Andre looked at him and then nodded at Sketch. Sketch followed him out of the apartment. "Stay with him, alright? Don't let him out of your site for any reason and don't leave him alone. You understand me, young-blood?" Andre said firmly.

Sketch nodded. "I won't."

Andre left quickly and hauled-ass over to the hospital. He had just gotten to the waiting room when he heard Tiffany going off.

Yani

"Mistaken identity?! Really! How the FUCK is it a case of mistaken identity when you hear him say on the video that he's a fucking detective! They put a hit on him because he didn't go along and cover up the dirty shit that was going on in the department!" she yelled. Shawn was trying to quiet her down. Ms. Keyona was beside herself with grief after seeing the video on the news of her son being gunned down. Deisha and Chanda were rubbing her back and talking to her as she puked and sobbed over a trash can.

Andre walked over to Tiffany quickly and grabbed her. "You need to close your mouth, Tiff." She looked at him with fire in her eyes as though she was two seconds away from fucking him up. He leaned over and talked to her in her ear. "We know it was a hit. They know it was a hit. The problem now is that the public sees it and their lies are about to fall apart. But you cannot rant and rave in here about what was done to him unless you want to end up like Dante's girlfriend."

Tiffany looked at him confused. "What do you mean?" she asked, though she had an idea what he was trying to say.

"She's dead." Andre said to her. "And the kid that recorded my son, your husband getting gunned down is fighting for his life right now because they tried to off him too. So before you fire off threats and what the fuck ever else you're spewing, close that pretty little mouth of yours and focus your attention and your energy on the baby you're carrying and your faith that Jamal will pull through this."

Tiffany nodded her head. She could still see the way Jamal's body jerked as he was getting shot and the way he fell into the glass door before hitting the ground. But she was all cried out and the only thing she could feel at that moment was fury as she thought back to how the cops tried to spin the mistaken identity story. "Jamal is back in surgery," she said to Andre.

"Okay. All we can do now is wait." They walked over to where Maurice and Shawn were sitting and sat down beside them.

"That shit was fucking foul," Shawn said as he shook his head.

"The city and the police department is going to have the mother of all law suits because of this. Not just from y'all, but the kid who recorded the video who was shot by the cops to." Maurice shook his head. "These fucking pigs supposed to serve and protect. But the only thing they're trying to protect are their own asses. They the main ones out here doing the crime. How you shoot a kid because you don't want the world to see that you tried to execute one of your own? The shit is mind boggling."

Yani

"Shawn Williams?" a man said as he looked around the waiting room. Shawn looked up and the man began walking over to him. "I was wondering if I could get a few words from you about the recent discovery into your brother's shooting?" the reporter asked politely.

Andre looked as though he was going to break the reporter's neck but Shawn stopped him.

"It's okay, Dad." Shawn said as he placed a hand on his father's chest to stop him. He looked at the reporter for a moment and then cleared his throat.

"I wish I could say that justice will be served for my brother and what was done to him. But the very people who are supposed to uphold the laws and fight for justice, broke those same laws when they targeted my brother," Shawn said as he trembled with grief.

"So you're not buying the mistaken identity spin the cops were trying to spew?" the reporter asked.

"Hell no. My brother's car was blown up the night before he was shot. Then he and his wife and our father were ambushed at his house that same night and when that didn't work, they targeted him while he was picking up ice-cream for his two-year-old son. How the fuck are we supposed to have faith that the system will handle this the right way when the system targeted him and marked him for death. Fuck the police!" Shawn spat angrily. Chanda came over to him and rubbed his back, trying to console him.

The reporter winced, but inside he was glad that he lied claiming to be a relative of Tiffany's so he could gain access to the waiting room that they were in. "I feel you on that. One last question, I don't want to take up too much of your time. "How is Jamal? Is he going to pull through?"

"He's back in surgery, but he was critical and flat-lined on us twice. So if he dies, the City of Philadelphia and the Philadelphia Police Department will have his blood on their hands. And you can quote me on all of that shit."

"Thank you for your time. I appreciate it," the reporter said before shaking Shawn's hand. He was about to turn away and then stopped. "I'm sorry, I know I said that was my last question, I just have one more and then I'll let you get back to your family. Do you know where the video came from? I heard rumors that it was from a kid but I haven't been able to confirm that information."

Andre interjected. "His name is Cyndrell. The cops shot him earlier trying to get the video from him. They would have shot his girlfriend as well if Detective Dante Smith was not there to save them. He's Detective Jamal Williams' partner."

Shawn looked at his father shocked that he said so much. Andre shrugged. "I ain't no snitch but fuck it. Too much done happened in the last 48 hours. Muthafucking heads need to roll. The department needs to be cleaned up, this shit needs to fucking end."

The reporter nodded his head in agreement. He then reached in his back pocket and gave both Shawn and Andre his business cards. "I hope your brother pulls through and I hope all parties responsible for the pain your family is going through right now are prosecuted to fullest extent of the law."

"Thank you," Shawn replied as he tucked the business card in his back pocket. The reporter left as quietly as he came and Shawn sat back down with Chanda. Moments later the doctors came over to them. They all stood up anxious to hear what the doctors had to say, but frightened all at the same time.

"We were able to remove the last of the fragments, however, the damage was still quite extensive. Right now, we have him sedated to minimize the pain. Really all we can do now is keep him comfortable and hope that his body will naturally heal itself. I wish I could tell you specifically what his chance are…" the doctor hesitated as he looked at everyone. "At best, I would say 30%. I truly am sorry," the doctor said sorrowfully.

"Can we see him?" Tiffany asked, trying to remain strong.

"Yes, we will move him to his room within the next half hour and then you all can sit with him, if you'd like."

"Thank you," Shawn replied. They fell silent as the doctor left the waiting room.

"30% is still a good chance," Ms. Keyona said with a sniff.

Andre shook his head. "Keys, he's dying. Our boy is dying," he told her as he put his arm around her.

"No, I won't accept that. He still here. He's still fighting. Jamal's never been a quitter and I don't think he will leave his wife and son and the baby he has on the way. No, not my boy." Keyona said defiantly. Andre squeezed her knowing it was going to be hard for her to accept that he was dying.

"He signed a DNR..." Tiffany said. "And he's in pain. I think if he had a choice between being in pain and being at peace, he would choose peace." Tears fell from her eyes as she said that.

"So what are you saying?" Shawn asked her.

Tiffany wiped her face. "I'm saying that if he flat-lines again..."

Ms. Keyona looked at her with fire in her eyes. "No! Absolutely not!" she spat.

Yani

"Mom, she's right. Reviving him again and again will only prolong his pain and we'll be doing it for a selfish reason; because we all still want him here with us. But we all know that he wouldn't want to be here like that," Shawn said to his mother. He put his arms around her and held her as she sobbed, crying and begging God to give him the strength to live.

"Maurice, if it's not too much for me to ask, can you get our son and bring him up here?" Tiffany asked.

Maurice stood up with Deisha. "Yeah, that's no problem. We'll be back soon." He and Deisha left the hospital.

"I need to make a run to check on D-Ball. See if he wants to come back to the hospital." Andre said as he stood up to leave.

"Wait… check on D-Ball? What happened?" Chanda asked.

Andre looked at them all and sighed. "His girlfriend was killed in their apartment. We found her right before I came here."

Shawn shook his head. "This shit is… this shit is fucking crazy!"

"Call me if anything changes," Andre said before heading out of the hospital as well.

23

Sergeant Rutkowski paced inside of his office almost in a panic mode when the news aired the video of Jamal's shooting that they tried desperately to confiscate as well as have the source neutralized. He knew that the heat was going to fall down on him since he failed to have Jamal taken out without any witnesses. He had to come up with a plan and fast. He figured if all else failed, he would take out whoever he could on his way down.

His phone rung and he froze when he looked at the caller ID and saw that it was Captain Bowser. He took a deep breath knowing that he couldn't decline or ignore the call. He answered the call in a surprisingly calm voice,

"This is Rutkowski."

"You wanna explain what the fuck happened?" Bowser asked in an intimidating voice.

"Sir," Rutkowski started.

Yani

"Don't speak!" Bowser said in a loud voice dripping in venom. Rutkowski quieted down. "You had a simple job, take out Williams and Dante swiftly and with no witnesses. Williams is hanging on by a thread, Dante has killed more people than you and now the video is out not to mention the news is reporting that the teenager who recorded Williams' shooting was shot by police earlier. Give me one good reason why I shouldn't have my guys put a bullet in your head right now for this kind of massive fuck up."

"I can still get to Dante," Rutkowski blurted out.

"How? And what's the point now?"

"The point being he wouldn't be able to testify. Not only can I get Dante, but I can finally have Andre taken out as well." Rutkowski said with a stutter.

Bowser tapped his fingers on the desk as he thought over what Rutkowski said.

"How do you plan to do that?" he asked.

"Just leave it to me. I promise, you won't be disappointed. I can get this back on track. The cops who shot Jamal are expendable. We can still move forward with our plan."

"You have until tonight to set this right or else your wife will need your dental records to identify your body." And with those words, Bowser hung up the phone.

Rutkowski closed his eyes as Bowser's threat hung in the air. He knew he had better deliver on his word because Bowser wasn't one who made idle threats. He dialed another number and waited patiently.

"You better be every fucking inch as good as you say you are. It's time to put the plan into motion, now." Rutkowski gave specific instructions to the person on the phone and then hung up. He sat down at his desk looking at a chess board that he had set up where he was playing himself. "Rook takes bishop pawn… Check."

24

D-Ball watched as Nicole's body was put in a body bag and zipped up. Sketch stood by his side as Andre instructed him to and waited with him while the cops did their investigating. When they were done, they gave Dante a business card advising him to come down to the precinct at his earliest convenience. Dante didn't say anything. He had murder on his mind except the problem was, he didn't know who the target was.

"You good man? Do you need anything?" Sketch asked him.

Dante wiped out his eyes and took a deep breath before nodding. "Yeah, I'm good man. I just need to take care of some shit, that's all."

"Well name it OG and I got you. You know I do," Sketch said as he followed D-Ball out of the apartment.

"Look, I know Andre told you to stay with me and keep an eye on me and shit, but I'm good. Just go back around the way and I'll holla at you later." D-Ball said to him.

"Look, even if Jamal's pops didn't tell me to stick by you, I'd still be here. You and Jamal are like my older brothers. Y'all always looked out for me in the streets and shit so it's only right that I return that favor, you feel me." Sketch insisted.

D-Ball thought about what he said and gave in, too mentally exhausted to argue or fight. They left out of the apartment complex just as Andre was pulling up.

"You good, young-blood?" Andre asked Dante. Dante shook his head as he walked over to the truck.

"Did you get to Tiff and them before they saw the footage?" Dante asked.

"Nah, they had just saw the footage when I got there. Jamal is out of surgery but it's still not looking good for him. They're giving him 30% but judging by the look on the doctor's face, I got a feeling that it's less than that." Andre explained.

"Wait, what…? I thought y'all said that Jamal was good?" Sketch asked looking from Andre to D-Ball confused.

"We were trying to stay positive," Andre shook his head not knowing what more he should say. His phone rang and he saw it was George. "Yeah?"

Yani

"Plans have changed. I managed to tap the phone of Sergeant Rutkowski who is the main one orchestrating all of this that's going on, they just named you and Dante as targets. They're going to try to take you both out and let the cops who shot Jamal go down on their own." George explained.

"Thanks for the heads up. We're on our way." Andre replied. He disconnected the call. "We need to make a run back to the safe house to round up on some things. George says we've been targeted. Let's move."

Dante jumped in the passenger side of the truck and pulled both of his guns, making sure they were both fully loaded. One only had half of a clip. He cursed under his breath when he saw he didn't have any more ammo on him.

"We can load up when we get there," Andre told him.

"What about me?" Sketch asked.

Andre looked at him for a second. "How old are you, young-blood?"

"I'm 26, sir." Sketch replied with confidence.

Andre looked him over for a second thinking maybe he should leave him behind but then thought they could use an extra man. He waved for him to get in the truck.

"Hold up one second. He jogged over to one of his friends who were about to leave. They exchanged a few words and then the guy passed him something. Sketch ran back to the truck and jumped in the back.

"What you got there?" Andre asked as he revved up the engine.

"My man's carry that heat!" Sketch grinned as he unwrapped the AK-47.

"Holy-shit, you ain't playing." Andre said as he pulled off.

"D-Ball told me he had some heat. I had to make sure my niggas were ready," Sketch replied.

"My man," D-Ball said as he reached in the back of the truck and gave Sketch a pound. Andre made his way over to the safe house so they could get ready for whatever was about to come their way.

Yani

24

Jamal was inside of his changing room at the beach house where he and Tiffany were scheduled to get married on the beach just before the sunset. Since neither of them were big on church, they thought it would be more real and intimate if they were married some place neutral. He was going through his suitcase, taking out the things that he needed to get ready when he heard something fall on the floor. He looked to see what it was and froze. Jamal stared for a moment at the ring he had given to Tamera almost twelve years prior. He sat down on the floor with his legs crossed as he held the ring between his fingers, looking at it and reflecting on the day he asked her to marry him. He remembered it was the night before she was killed and his heart began to ache.

"Remember this?" he asked. Tamera looked at her hand and smiled. "Thought I forgot about it, didn't you? I still want you to have it. But not just as my girl. I want you as my wife," Jamal asked nervously.

"Jamal…" Tamera whispered as she looked at him.

"I know we're young and no I'm not just asking you because you're carrying my baby. And even though you won't tell me, I know you love me. And I love you more than anything. I meant it when I said you were it for me. And if it's the ring, we can get another one…" Jamal rambled.

Tamera shushed him. "Yes babe. Yes, I will. You're it for me too," she said softly.

"You will?" Jamal asked again. Tamera nodded her head. Jamal kissed her passionately.

"Damn…" Jamal said to himself as he shook his head. He was so deep in thought, reflecting on one of the last moments he was with Tamera that he didn't hear Maurice when he came in the room.

"Nigga, what are you doing sitting on the damn floor like you don't have a wedding to get to in gee…" he stopped to looked at his watch. "…twenty minutes?"

Jamal still wasn't paying Maurice any mind as he was still thinking about Tamera and the time she told him she loved him finally.

"You know, that's the first time you ever said that to me," Jamal said to Tamera as he looked at her.

"But you know I meant it every day…" she said in return.

Maurice looked at Jamal closely to see what he was holding and then fell silent.

Yani

"August 15th 2002 changed my life forever…" Jamal said to Maurice as he continued to look at the ring.

"That day changed all of our lives," Maurice said in return.

"Yeah, it showed us just how fucked up life really can be. I swear, I lost whatever little faith I had in God that day. All I kept wondering for years after that was if there really is a God, how the fuck could he let something like that happen to Tammy while she was pregnant? How?" Jamal asked.

Maurice could hear the pain and anger in his voice. He waited a moment before responding. "You know, I'm not one to get preachy because I'm not about that church life myself. The only reason I agreed to a church wedding is because it was what Deisha wanted and I love her so whatever she wants, if I can give it to her, she can have it. But what happened to Tammy…" Maurice trailed off trying to pick his words carefully knowing that it was a very sensitive topic for Jamal. "That had to happen," he said finally. Jamal looked up at him as though what he said was ridiculous. "Hear me out, 'Mal, before you start snapping. After Raheem was killed, you fell so deep in the streets, it seemed like nothing would pull you out. You were shot, you stayed in the streets. Your brother was shot, you stayed in the streets. You found out Samir shot your father and had you thinking for years he had your back when really he didn't give a fuck about you beyond what you could do for him, and you were still in the streets. Tamera got pregnant, and you stayed in the streets."

Jamal cut him off becoming pissed. "What the fuck is your point?"

"My point is all of the shit that was happening to you and happening around you, you stayed in the streets. If Tamera had not been killed and you walked away from that beef with Samir untouched, you wouldn't have learned anything. And more than likely you would have went right back to the streets because that's all you knew. So as fucked up as it is that she was killed the way she was and y'all baby died with her, a lesson had to be learned. And it was one of the harshest muthafucking lessons that I wouldn't wish on my worst enemy. But guess what, man? Look what you've done with your life since then. You're on the right side of the law, you cleaned up one of the most corrupt police departments on the east coast, you have a son and a woman that loves you just as much if not more than Tamera did. She's everything you need, man. So don't feel like you were robbed when Tammy was killed. You were given a second chance at living life right."

"But it should've been with her." Jamal mumbled as he fought back his tears.

"So what, you're going to cancel your wedding behind hurt feelings from twelve-year-old pain? Punish yourself. Come on, man. Come on! Tammy wouldn't want that for you and you know it."

Jamal thought on his best friend's words as he held onto the ring a little longer. He then smirked. "Deisha is starting to wear off on you, nigga. You sound like a male version of Oprah." They both burst out

Yani

laughing as Maurice helped Jamal get up off of the floor. "Fucking fix my life Iyanla Vanzant." They laughed some more.

"Nigga you got jokes. Get your tux on before Tiff thinks you left her at the altar." Maurice said as he left the room Jamal was in.

Jamal looked at himself in the mirror. "If you can stand me forever, can I have you forever?" he said as he thought over part of his wedding vows. He took a deep breath and began to get himself ready for the biggest day of his life…

***

Ms. Keyona leaned over Jamal and gave him a long lingering kiss. "Jamal, baby, if you can hear me, I want you to know I love you. I love you with all of my heart and I'm begging you honey to please keep fighting. I'm sorry if I sound selfish but I'm not asking for me. I'm asking for your wife and for Jamir and for the beautiful baby that you have on the way. I know you may be tired and it would be a lot easier and peaceful for you to let go but please, please don't give up. Keep fighting. You've always been strong… just please don't give up." Ms. Keyona sniffed back her tears and kissed her son again before leaving the room unable to look at her son laying in the hospital bed the way that he was.

25

Andre pulled up to the safe house and got out of the truck. Sketch was about to get out with them but Andre stopped him.

"You stay here, young-blood. We'll be out in a little bit," he told him. Sketch was disappointed, feeling like Andre didn't trust his ability to be a rider. But he didn't argue. Not wanting to be seen as a whining kid, he sat in the back of the truck like he was told.

They walked into the safe house and saw Felix and George eating Chinese Food.

"Where's mine?" Andre asked, half serious.

George stopped in mid-bite feeling selfish. "My bad. I got a shrimp roll over here if you wanna get down with that."

Andre waved him off. "Nah, I'm just fucking with you." He went to the back of the room with D-Ball and they began loading up on ammo.

Yani

Felix came downstairs and went over to D-Ball. "I'm sorry about your girl," he said sympathetically.

D-Ball shrugged. "Thanks." He slammed a clip in a gun and then pulled one of Andre's shotguns, loading the shells in as Andre strapped up as well. The silence felt awkward to Felix so he went over to George.

"Anything new come in?" he asked.

George shook his head as he looked over his monitors. He then frowned and grabbed his stomach. "Damn, what the hell was in that shrimp and broccoli?"

Felix chuckled. "For starters, it damn sure wasn't shrimp."

"Can you keep an eye on the monitors. I gotta take a shit," George grimaced as he made his way over to the steps.

Felix laughed at him. "That was too much information." He could still hear George groaning as he made his way up the stairs.

Sketch was in the truck texting a cutie that he'd given his number to earlier that day. He was so into their conversation that he didn't notice the five guys get out of a car in front of him and head over to the door of the safe house that D-Ball, Andre, Felix and George were in. Because the windows to the truck were dark with tint, he could not be seen either.

One of the guys kicked the door in and wasted no time spraying with his Ak-47. He hit the monitors and almost hit Felix had he not been quick with his dive behind an island that separated the two rooms. He cursed himself as he covered his head as he was without a weapon. The other guys opened fire in D-Ball and Andre's direction. D-Ball threw himself over a table and flipped it on the side to catch the bullets coming his way. They were out-numbered with no real place to hide. Andre was crouched in a corner behind a tiny wall near the stairs. He saw Felix crouched down and slid a gun over to him. The gunmen let off shots in his directions.

"I'm not dying today. Fuck this shit!" D-Ball growled. He waited until it sounded like they were about to reload and he and Andre both began firing at them. Two of the gunmen returned fire hitting Andre.

D-Ball cursed when he ran out of bullets. He reached for the shotgun when he heard more gunfire. Sketch heard the action from inside of the truck and came in as back up. He let off gunfire from his Ak-47, slicing into two of the gunmen. The shots startled the other three. They turned in his direction giving D-Ball a chance to grab the shotgun.

"Sketch, move!" D-Ball yelled as he took advantage of the pump action. The loud boom of the shotgun blasts sounded off through the downstairs as he caught one in the back, the gunfire blowing through his chest knocking him to the ground. He caught the other in the side and Felix shot the last one in the head. When everything went quiet, Felix scrambled upstairs to check on George. D-Ball went over to Andre where he was laying on the floor.

"Five times. Five muthafucking times, these niggas still can't seem to get it right." Andre groaned as he struggled to sit up.

D-Ball let out a sigh of relief as he helped Andre to stand up. "God bless your vest," he said to him.

"Shit, I put two on just in case. I saw what they did to my boy." Andre said in return. He then looked at Sketch who looked shaken up. "Good looking, young-blood. Aren't you glad I told you to stay in the truck."

George was upstairs hiding in the tub with his arms over his head.

"George, you okay?" Felix asked him. George was so shaken up he didn't realize his lip was busted from when he dove into the tub. Felix grabbed his arm and pulled him up. "Come on, let's get the fuck out of here before they send another hit."

George climbed from the tub trying to wipe the tears from his face before the rest of the guys could see that he had been crying like a bitch. When he got downstairs and saw that the bulk of his equipment had been destroyed his heart sank into his stomach.

"They destroyed the monitors but the dumb-asses didn't touch the hard-drives, so it's not much of a loss," Felix told George to ease his anguish. George nodded at him as he began to gather everything up. Andre stared at him for a moment but didn't say anything. They gathered up as much as they could and hurried up and left the safe house.

"They're not going to stop coming for us." Andre said to D-Ball.

D-Ball was quiet as he thought about what Andre said. "Yeah, I know," he said after a moment.

"Where to now?" Felix replied.

"Well first things first. You my friend, will be rejoining the living. A reporter gave me his business card. I think it's time we give them an exclusive and tell what the fuck is going on in Philly with the corrupt police force and what they're trying to do. But if we're going to do it, we need to do it now otherwise we won't make to Monday," Andre replied.

Felix was stunned at Andre's plan. "How do you figure that's going to work?"

"Do you want to keep ducking and dodging bullets? Afraid to get in your car and turn the key in the ignition, wondering if there is a bomb waiting to blow you the fuck up? I sure as fuck don't. You know just as well as I do that it's kill or be killed and I personally prefer to do the killing." Andre spat as he drove towards the expressway.

"Fucking right with that shit," Sketch replied.

"Shit…" Felix frowned. It had to be another way out of this.

26

While Ms. Matthews was receiving wonderful news that her son was expected to make a full recovery, Jamal's condition was worsening. Tiffany prayed that Maurice made it back in time for their son to have the chance to see his father before he passed away.

"Hold on, Jamal. Hold on just a little longer, baby," Tiffany begged as she held his hand which were beginning to feel extremely cold. Shawn sat in a chair by the door with Chanda sitting on his lap stroking the back of his head. Ms. Keyona didn't come back in the room. She was there when Jamal took his first breath. She couldn't bear to see him take his last.

***

Jamal and Shawn stood in the room after getting dressed. Had Shawn been a little bit darker, they would have been able to pass as twins. Shawn adjusted his older brother's bow-tie.

Yani

"I never pegged you to be a Hugo Boss kinda man," Shawn smirked.

Jamal tugged at the bow-tie that felt uncomfortable. "Yeah, I let Tiff pick out the tux and the groomsman stuff. Her eye for this kind of shit is better than mine." He and Shawn laughed together as Maurice was coming in the room with Shawn's son Dre who was going to be the ring bearer. The photographer came in behind them and took some pictures as they joked around.

They made their way out to the altar that was set up on the beach with a white, silky pathway that led from the altar to the beach house that Tiffany was going to be coming from. White orchids along with white and pink roses adorned the altar along with the archway that Jamal and his groomsmen stood under waiting for her. He was nervous and took multiple deep breaths to keep himself calm. His mother smiled at him and gave him a thumbs up. He smiled at her and his father in return.

Musiq Soul Child's "So Beautiful" began to play with Deisha and Maurice coming down the aisle first. Tiffany's best friend Amber came down with another grooms' man and then Shawn and Chanda came down the aisle. The doors closed and Jamal closed his eyes as his anticipation to see his future wife grew. He opened them just as the beach house doors opened...

***

"What's happening?" Tiffany panicked as the doctors rushed into Jamal's room when the machines that he was hooked up to began to alarm them that he was coding.

One of the doctors practically pushed her to the side as they rushed to assist him. Shawn stood up to see what was going on.

"He's in V-Fib," one of the doctors said. "Charge to 250." Tiffany clenched her hands into fist trying not to scream in the room all the while praying that God saved her husband. She watched Jamal's body jerk as they shocked him.

"Nothing," one of the other doctors said. "Resume CPR."

"Tiff, what are you doing?" Shawn said to her, thinking that they agreed they would let him go. "Tiff?" Shawn shouted to her.

"Just wait!" Tiffany screamed at him with tears in her eyes. She watched as they resumed CPR, trying desperately to save Jamal's life…

***

Yani

The beach house doors opened and Jamal watched his future wife looking angelic in her white strapless wedding gown with her veil covering her face. The small crowd of guests stood up to salute her. Her father had passed away in the beginning of their relationship so her nephew agreed to walk her down the aisle. She hooked her arm into his and they walked down the aisle slowly to the beat of the music. Jamal was overwhelmed with how beautiful she looked as she strutted towards him. He was absolutely positive that Tiffany was the perfect woman for him and he wanted to spend the rest of his life with her…

***

"Push one more round of epi," the doctor who was doing compressions on Jamal said. The paddles were charged once more.

"Please Jamal…" Tiffany said softly as her tears stained her cheeks. "Please…"

The paddles were placed on Jamal once more causing his body to jerk when they shocked him. Tiffany closed her eyes and waited asking God for a miracle one last time…

***

Jamal extended his hand when she made it down the aisle and helped her step up to the altar where they were to be married. He reached for the veil that covered her face and lift it up and it was as if everything and everyone disappeared.

Her beauty was beyond what he could recall as he stared at her in disbelief looking from her beautiful, chestnut brown eyes to her smooth sandy brown skin that held an angelic glow. He was at a loss for words as he stared at her and she stared at him.

"If you can stand me forever, can I have you forever?" Tamera said to him in a soft voice.

Jamal was frozen as he looked into Tamera's eyes. He hesitantly put his hand up to her face feeling the need to touch her, to see if she was real, to feel the heat from her skin touch his hand after dreaming of her for so many years and yearning for one last chance to touch her, hold her, kiss her, smell her. When his hand touched her face, and she was still there in front of him, he exhaled. Tamera closed her eyes as she felt his hand caress her cheek before running through her long dark hair. Jamal held her hand and put it to his face to feel her and feeling her brought tears to his eyes. He kissed her softly at first, like the many times they had kissed in high-school and then kissed her more deeply with every ounce of passion he had inside of him. He pulled her body close to him, hugging her as he breathed in Tamera's scent.

"I love you, Jamal," she said as she looked him in his eyes…

***

The doctors waited to see if they would get a heartbeat but didn't hear anything. The room held the long humming sound of the monitors as Jamal flat-lined and they were unable to bring him back around.

"Time of death…" one of the doctors began to say.

"NO!" Tiffany said. "Don't say it in here, please. Just get out! Get out!!" Tiffany screamed at the doctors before choking on her sobs. One of the doctors turned the monitor off to stop the humming sound and they cleared out of the room. Tiffany laid her head on his hand and sobbed loudly. She cried harder than she had ever done in her life. Everything in her body hurt and ached. She cursed God for robbing her of her husband and father of her children. She screamed and cried before collapsing to her knees.

Chanda sat in the chair with her hands to her face crying as well. Shawn went over to Tiffany and tried to help her up but she wouldn't budge, her grief paralyzing her. He pulled her up in his arms and held her as she cried.

Maurice had just arrived with Jamir, stuck in traffic behind a nasty car accident for over 45 minutes. Hearing Tiffany screaming and crying in the room let him know that his best friend was gone.

"Can I see my daddy now?" Jamir asked as he looked up at Maurice.

Maurice looked down at him not sure what to say. Instead he picked him up and walked him away from the room Jamal was in so he couldn't hear his mother's grief.

Tiffany let Shawn go and ran her hands over Jamal's face. "It's okay, baby," she whimpered. She kissed him softly on his lips and stroked his head. "Thank you for loving me." She stood up to walk away when she heard a loud gasp followed behind a choking cough.

Tiffany turned back around towards Jamal and ran back to him.

"Jamal, Jamal? Can you hear me?" Tiffany said as she cradled his head.

Shawn looked at him in disbelief and then snatched the door open. "We need a doctor in here! Somebody get in here!"

Doctors rushed down the hall and into the room.

"How in the hell?" one of the doctors asked in disbelief. They attended to Jamal as he continued to cough.

"Tammy…" he murmured after he was able to get a breath. His eyes fluttered as the doctors checked his vitals and shined a light in his eyes.

Tiffany looked at him and then looked at Shawn to see if he heard what she heard. Shawn returned the same look.

"This is… this is unbelievable. In my twenty years as a doctor, I've seen some pretty amazing things but this… this is probably the only one that I would classify as a miracle. Blood pressure is normal, pulse is steady… this is fucking incredible!" the doctor exclaimed.

Shawn hugged Chanda and they both hugged Tiffany as her tears of grief changed to joy and relief. She let Shawn go and rushed to Jamal's side. Jamal looked at her with tired eyes. She grabbed his hand and kissed it.

"You better had came back. I was about to kick your little dead ass in here," she said with a smile.

Jamal smiled weakly at her and then looked at his brother. Shawn nodded at him and he nodded in return.

27

During the time Jamal spent in the hospital recuperating, things were happening quickly. Captain Bowser of the Philadelphia Police Department had been found in his car shot in the head. His death was ruled a suicide after a note had been found next to him.

The cops who had not been taken out by D-Ball were all indicted on attempted murder charges for Jamal. They were also charged with the attempted murder of Dante Smith in relation to Jamal's car that exploded as well as the attempted murder of Cyndrell Matthews. They each plead not guilty.

Jamal was sitting in his room his last night at the hospital when he heard a knock at his door.

"Come in!" he called out to them. The door opened and a young man came in that Jamal had not seen before. His arm was in a sling and he looked nervous. "Can I help you?" Jamal asked as he positioned himself in his hospital bed and turned on ESPN so he could watch Shawn's game against the Golden State Warriors.

"Detective Williams…" the young man started.

"You can call me Jamal," he said in return.

"I'm sorry. Jamal… my name is Cyndrell Matthews. I don't mean to bother you. I just wanted to shake hands with a legend… if that's okay."

Jamal smiled at him, familiar with his name after hearing it so much in the news. He extended his hand for Cyndrell to shake it. "I'm not a legend. I'm just really lucky. Actually, I want to thank you for that."

"Thank me for what?" Cyndrell asked with a raised eyebrow.

"You recorded what happened to me. You risked your life to do what was right. Not a lot of guys your age would have been level headed and quick thinking enough or smart enough to do what you did. I heard you were jumping from rooftops to keep the cops from getting that recording from you," Jamal said with a grin.

Cyndrell laughed and rubbed his neck nervously. "Yeah, I was out. I knew what was up."

Jamal nodded his head. He looked at the young man and it was something about him that reminded him of himself when he was that age. He could tell that something was troubling him. "Something wrong?" he asked.

Cyndrell took a deep breath. "People at school, teachers kissing my ass… my fault," he apologized for cursing. Jamal waved him off. "But yeah, the teachers all kissing my ass calling me a hero, trying to get me to join a mentoring program and honestly, I don't think it's because they think I'm a good kid that did something brave because some of those niggas was texting telling me to turn myself in when they thought I was the one who robbed the 7-11 you were shot in front of. I really think it's because they heard about the 20 million-dollar lawsuit my mom launched against the city and the police department. Now it seems like they looking at me like they see dollar signs and not Cyndrell."

Jamal nodded his head. "Yeah… niggas are grimy. But don't let that change who you are. You keep doing your thing. Stay in school. Stay focused…"

"My girlfriend is pregnant," Cyndrell blurted out. Jamal took a double take at him. "She's scared. Shit, I'm scared. I don't know what to tell my mom. She doesn't know what to tell her parents. My father is dead, it's just me and my moms and I didn't know who to talk to. I mean at first I figured it'll be okay because the city probably will settle soon and I can help take care of my seed and still go to college. But then I heard that I won't get the money 'til I'm 21 and I'm like damn, I can't have my kid struggling for four years."

Jamal was at a loss for words as the young man spilled his guts to him. He at first wondered why Cyndrell came to him to talk. He wondered why he didn't go to his friends. But then he remembered what the young man said about his father being dead and he thought back to when he believed his father was dead at the age of 16 and figured most of his friends were probably knuckle-heads not doing shit with their lives.

"When I was 18, I got my girlfriend pregnant," Jamal said to Cyndrell. "I was a knuckle-head back then, in and out of trouble. I used to sell drugs, was shot when I was 17. But dealing with her pulled me away from the trouble and when I got her pregnant, I already had a job. I just started putting more of my money to the side to make sure I could offer her more than excuses; you know what I'm saying? You seem like a responsible young man. Sometimes shit happens. But don't let this turn you into a coward. Be a man and talk to her parents with her. Let them know what your plans are for their daughter and what you're willing to do to make sure both her and the baby are taken care of." Jamal schooled him.

"What if I can't do it? Like what if I can't find a job?" Cyndrell asked sounding like he was beginning to panic.

"What do you do besides school? You play sports?" Jamal asked him

"I box," Cyndrell said confidently.

Jamal nodded his head at him. "Are you any good?"

"Hell yeah. These niggas don't bother with me in the streets cause they ain't trying to catch these hands," Cyndrell said arrogantly.

"Are you planning on going pro?"

"I mean, I wanted to. But I figured if I couldn't then I would take up electrical engineering. I like physics and shit like that so…" Cyndrell shrugged his shoulders.

"Well then you're already on the right path because you have a plan and a backup plan. But this is what I want you to do," Jamal reached on the table that was near his hospital bed and grabbed a pen and a piece of paper. He scribbled down something quickly. "I want you to call this guy. His name is Skip. He owns a barber shop in West Oaklane off of Ogontz and Tulpehockon. Tell him I sent you for a job and he'll hook you up. Now you gotta be willing to listen and learn. But Skip will look out on the strength of my name and also because you put your neck on the line to help me. Where I come from…"

Cyndrell finished his sentence. "You look out for the people who show you love." They smiled at each other. Cyndrell took the paper from him and tucked it in his pocket. "Thanks Jamal, I appreciate it."

"No problem. I put my number on there also. If you ever need to talk or just need to clear your head or whatever, hit me up." Jamal glanced up and threw his fist in the air when he saw his brother Shawn dunk on Andre Iguodala. "That's what the fuck I'm talking about, Shawn!" Jamal exclaimed. Cyndrell looked at the TV.

"Yeah, I like watching him play. That's Shawn Williams… Wait… is that your brother?!"

Jamal nodded his head with a smile. "That's my younger brother."

"Oh shit! I love that nigga, yo! No homo." He and Jamal laughed. "That's crazy!" Cyndrell took his phone out and checked the time. "I gotta get home. Thanks for listening. I appreciate it."

"Anytime," Jamal said in return. Cyndrell left and closed the door behind him.

Rutkowski was sitting in his office writing up some paperwork. In all of the drama that went down with the cops getting indicted for Jamal's shooting, he was one of the only ones who walked away unscathed. He heard a tap at his door and looked up.

"Come in," he said.

George came into his office and stood by the door. "You have something for me?"

Rutkowski looked up at him as though he was contemplating something. He then reached in his desk drawer and tossed an envelope at him.

George opened it up and looked inside. He then looked at Rutkowski angrily. "This isn't what we agreed on."

"You think I don't know that you tipped Andre and Dante off about Bowser and what was going on in this precinct. What were you trying to do, get brownie points?" Rutkowski sneered. He reached in his drawer and pulled another envelope out and handed it to George. "Those are the results. 99.999% positive that Andre Williams is your father. What I don't understand is, for you to be such a fucking genius, why didn't you get the results yourself?" George didn't respond. Instead he looked at the results from the DNA test that he had Rutkowski run for him. "How long do you think Andre will let you live once he finds out you double crossed them to save that whore of a mother of yours?"

"You watch your muthafucking mouth," George glared at him. Rutkowski smiled. "He won't find out. And even if he did, he would never kill his own son." George said confidently as he put the paper work in his duffle bag.

Rutkowski nodded his head. "Maybe he won't, but I highly doubt Dante will be so forgiving or Jamal for that matter seeing as though you helped orchestrate his shooting."

"Where's my mother?" George asked.

"Keep your phone near you. There's some more work that needs to be done, okay Georgie?" Rutkowski said with a smirk.

George stared at him angrily for a moment and then left out of his office. He hurried over to the elevator looking around to make sure no one saw him and then got on when it got to his floor.

Andre stepped from a shadowy corner near Rutkowski's office shocked over what he heard.

"Did you get that?" Andre asked quietly into his blue-tooth.

"Yeah… I got that." Felix said feeling the same shock that Andre felt. The plan was for Andre to kill Rutkowski once he learned he was also behind the car bomb and the shooting that almost killed Jamal. He was shocked when he saw George heading to Rutkowski's office ahead of him.

He then thought back to how eager George was to meet him and how excited he was to meet Jamal. And then, as though it were a movie playing back in his head, Andre began piecing things together for himself…

"Hey Jamal, let me see your phone to make sure nobody put a tap on it," George requested as he swirled around in his desk chair.

Jamal passed him his phone. "Good looking," he said in return.

George took his phone and turned to his computer. Instead of making sure there was no tap placed on Jamal's phone, he planted a virus on it, blocking it from being able to make calls or receive them. When he was finished, he gave the phone back to Jamal.

"You're good," he said casually. Jamal nodded his head as he put his phone back in his pocket…

He then thought about what D-Ball said when the video came into his phone of Nicole and the men who murdered her, men who were wearing the same mask he wore when he killed Officer Daniels.

"You said the cameras were blacked out!" D-Ball practically growled as he held George by the scruff of his neck.

"They were…" George squealed.

"Then how the fuck them niggas wearing the same fucking mask I wore when I took out Daniels!? How bitch!?"

"I don't know…" George continued to squeal.

Andre stared in the direction that George went in in disbelief as his mind continued to play the movie in flashes in his head.

"It's an honor to finally meet you, Mr. Williams. I've heard so much about you," George said as he shook Andre's hand.

"Is that right? You look familiar. Do I know you from somewhere?" Andre asked as he peered at the young hacker.

George hesitated for a moment as though he was thinking of a response. "I doubt it," he finally said.

Andre's eyes grew wide as it finally occurred to him why George looked so familiar and it clicked who his mother was. A woman that he paired up with while he was in California on assignment who he had become fond of and had taken to with the hope that it would help ease the pain of being away from Keyona and his sons. He always wondered why she had been suddenly reassigned and now he knew why. The tops knew she was pregnant with his child.

It all became clear that as George had them thinking that he was hacking and watching things that was going on, he really was tipping off the police department about what they were doing, which is how they found the safe house both times, how they got to Nicole and how they got to Jamal. George helped set them up. Judging by the conversation that Andre eavesdropped on, it had something to do with his mother and what was done to her.

Everything inside of Andre told him to kill George, but who his mother was and what she had to do with things made him curious to know exactly what the fuck was going on. He waited until the elevator let George off before calling it back to his floor so he could leave. The "tops" had some explaining to do, or there was going to be hell to pay…

Yani

Epilogue:

A Thug's Life Revisited: Game Over

Six months had passed since the day Jamal nearly died. Tiffany was well into her pregnancy and they were in the back of their house planting collard greens and corn on the cob. Jamir was playing with a new remote control car that Jamal had bought for his third birthday.

It was a beautiful, spring day. The pink rose bush that sat in the far end of their backyard was already blossoming. Despite her back killing her from the pregnancy weight, Tiffany was in a great mood. She decided to take a break and eased into her patio chair underneath the oak tree in the shade.

Jamal smiled at her as he passed her a cold bottle of Clear Fruit flavored water.

"Don't go too far, Mir!" Tiffany called to their son.

"I won't!" Jamir hollered back.

Jamal knelt down and kissed her stomach before rubbing it. "She's going to be bigger than Jamir, watch," he said with a grin.

Tiffany grinned with him before popping him on the arm. "You keep on saying that. You must don't want me to have any walls." They both burst out laughing.

"Nah, then I'll just get you some Yoni eggs to keep my punani just how I like it." Jamal said before licking his tongue at her in a suggestive manner.

Tiffany shook her head at him. "You are so nasty."

"You like it though," Jamal teased. He leaned over top of her and kissed her. He looked her in her eyes but it was something about the way she looked at him that seemed off. "What's wrong, babe?"

Tiffany played with her water bottle as she thought over her response. "When you were shot and the doctors had to revive you…" Tiffany hesitated for a moment. "…when you came to, you called out Tammy's name." She looked at him to gauge his response.

Jamal had hoped that the conversation never came up. He shook his head. "I can't explain that Tiff because it's still a little odd to me. I don't remember dreaming while I was out or sedated or whatever the fuck was happening to me. It was more like I was reliving moments, like when I surprised you with the house, when you went into labor and when we got married." It was Jamal who hesitated this time hoping that he didn't offend his wife with what he said next. "It was the memory of our wedding when things got a little crazy. You were coming down the aisle with your nephew Tyreese just like on the actual day except when I took your hand and pulled back your veil, it wasn't you. It was her. It was Tammy."

Tiffany frowned at him and then shook her head. "What do you mean?"

"She was standing in front of me in a wedding dress just as real as you are right now sitting in front of me. I could touch her, I could smell her. It felt so real that I wasn't sure if it was a dream or a memory anymore."

Tiffany looked away from him and squinted. Apart of her was hurt and another part of her was angry. Through it all, she tried to be understanding. "That must have been when you died. When they were ready to call your time of death. They say when you die, you see loved ones that passed before you. Maybe you really did see her. But Jamal… it almost sounds like you wish you'd married her instead of me."

Jamal sighed. "Tiff, I can't even believe you said that. She was the first girl I fell in love with and she was murdered because of me while carrying my baby. So of course fourteen years late there's still going to be some pain there. But that doesn't change the fact that I'm in love with you, now. You're my wife and my best friend. I said her name because I saw her. It's no different than the times I would wake up in a cold sweat saying her name because I would have the same dream about her again and again. So don't think that and don't let me hear you say some shit like that again either." Jamal said firmly. He kissed her briefly and she smiled.

"I love it when you're so bossy." Tiffany said with a grin.

"Yeah, that's why your ass pregnant again," Jamal chuckled as he stood up. "You want some lunch?"

"Yeah, can you fix me and Jamir a buffalo chicken breast and turkey ham sandwich, please? Mmm with some cookies." Tiffany said as she rubbed her hands together.

"Alright. 'Mir! Come on and get some lunch, young bol." Jamal called to his son as he started walking towards the back door. His son didn't respond so he called him again. "Mir-Mir, come on. Bring your car."

Tiffany frowned and leaned over in her chair to see if he was near the front of the house. Jamal closed the storm door and walked over to the side of the house.

"Come on, Mir. We can play hide-n-seek after you eat lunch. Jamir?"

Yani

Tiffany got out of her chair getting a nagging feeling in her stomach. She placed a hand on her stomach and began following behind Jamal.

"Jamir!" Tiffany called out her son's name when she didn't see him. Jamal saw his remote control and the car but didn't see him either. He picked it up and looked around, also getting a bad feeling.

"Check the house," Tiffany said trying not to panic. Jamal ran in the house calling his son's name. Tiffany checked the inside of their Nissan Pathfinder to see if he was hiding in there. Her eyes teared up as she turned from left to right, calling her son's name.

Jamal checked in the closets, under the dining room and kitchen table. He then ran upstairs skipping the steps two at a time and checked the closets up there as well as the bedrooms, under the beds and in the bathroom. His son was no-where to be found.

Tiffany stopped an older woman who was walking her dog. "Excuse me Miss, did you see a little boy…?" she asked the woman as she described her son and what he was wearing. The older woman shook her head "no". Jamal came back out the house.

"Was he in there?" Tiffany asked as she trembled.

"No. He was right here. We were only talking for two minutes," Jamal said as he pulled his cell phone.

"It only takes two minutes!" Tiffany yelled as the tears began to spill out. She put her hand to her mouth and looked around before calling her son's name again.

Jamal pulled Tiffany close to him as he thought of who he could call, still not trusting the police department that much.

"Where is he?" Tiffany practically screamed.

"We'll find him, babe. I promise." Jamal assured her as he hugged her.

His phone rang as he was about to call his father. He answered quickly. "Hello?"

"Jamal Williams?" a distorted voice said into the phone.

Jamal hesitated. "Yeah?"

"We have your son. If you want him back alive, if you ever want to see him again other than to identify his tiny, little body, listen closely and do exactly what the fuck I say. No police, don't even fucking think about calling the cops or this little bastard is dead. Understand?" the person on the other end of the phone said.

"Where's my son?" Jamal asked.

"Stay by the phone and wait for instructions. Otherwise, you'll find him when you smell him." The call was disconnected and Jamal looked at his phone. He tried to call the number back but it sounded like it went to a fax machine.

"Who was that?" Tiffany asked. Jamal didn't answer her. Moments later, a small video clip came through on his phone. It was of his son blind folded with head-phones on and a gun pointed closely to his head as he sat in the back of a car.

"Fuck…" Jamal said as his face frowned up. His mind raced as he thought of what he should do or what he could do. The police weren't an option because he couldn't trust them. For all he knew, they were the ones who had his son.

Jamal looked at his wife. "They took our son…"

Coming Soon- Something Thuggish This Way Comes

Novels by Yani

A Thug's Redemption Series

Obsessive Intimacies   Love's Deadly Masquerade

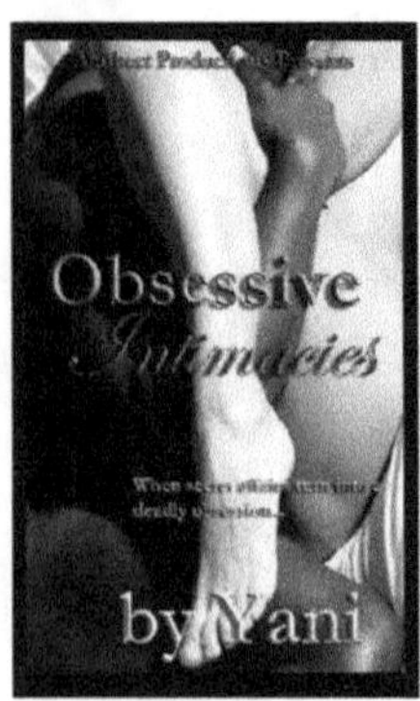

<u>Licked into *Submission* **Preview**</u>

1

Shadows of the candle's flames danced on the wall as the scent of coconut oil and Jasmine scented flowers filtered throughout the room. Those scents were being out-done by the over powering aroma of sex infiltrating my bedroom.

J-Holiday crooned through the surround sound in my bedroom and I could curse his fine ass right now because I was definitely being put to bed… bed… bed. I promised myself that I wouldn't do this again, that I wouldn't allow myself to be seduced into being Carmelo's bed wench again because it didn't seem like the situationship that we had gotten tangled up in was a good idea. For some reason, R-Kelly is in my head right now because my mind was definitely telling me no. But my body… yeah, my body was telling… no screaming yes. Yes! Lawd, yes. Hell my body was speaking languages I'd never known after feeling Carmelo's warm wet tongue twirling, swirling and flickering back and forth across my clit to the beat of J-Holiday's song *"Bed"*.

My hands were tied with silken white scarves to the maple wood head board attached to my king sized bed. While I usually don't allow myself to be in this kind of state of vulnerability, the way Carmelo's pussy licking technique was set up, I didn't mind being vulnerable for one more night. And ahhh, there lies the problem. But that explanation is going to have to wait… one… minute…

Damn, Carmelo just pushed my legs back to my chest with his arms hooked around them so I can't run and his tongue is giving my pussy the tongue thrashing that it craves. My back arched against the black silk sheets and my arms yanked at the silken scarves wanting desperately to grab ahold of something, preferably the back of his head so I could grind my pussy all over his mouth. Not being able to do so was driving me mad.

I felt his fingers exploring my tight wetness, going in and out as he licked and sucked me into an orgasmic heaven and my God did I cum so hard once he began sucking on my clit and pushing his fingers in deep enough to hit my G-Spot. I don't know what was hotter, the fact that he could do with his fingers what most men can't do with their dicks or the devilish

Yani

look on his face as he stared at me while he lapped up my cunt juices like a cat would lap up cream.

I breathed deeply as I looked down at him, sure that he was going to untie me so I could return the favor. As the saying goes: one good lick deserves another and he definitely deserved to have his dick devoured whole. But instead, he positioned himself on his knees in between my legs as he held his thick, black rock hard nine-inch dick. I stared like a wide eyed child seeing a plethora of gifts under the Christmas tree. And in my mind I was thinking *"Oh shit, he brought dick with him, too!"* Life is good…

Carmelo grabbed my legs and put them up over his shoulders never taking his eyes off of me, which always made the sex between us so damn hot. These damn silk scarves were in the way. I wanted to grab the dick myself and put it in. I wanted to grab his ass and feel those tight, muscular glutes flexing as he pumped that big, black ding-a-ling deep inside of my tight, wet tunnel. But he wanted me to take it how he gave it. And judging by that hungry, animalistic look in his eyes, he was about to beat this pussy up something fierce.

I gasped when I felt him enter me slow and deep. With my ankles atop his shoulders, he pushed my knees back to my chest and gave me a long, wet, sensuous kiss, with his tongue dancing around my mouth so I could taste the sweet flavor of my nectar on him. And then he went to work. I lost count of how many times I came. By the time it was over, I was sure I was about to slip into an orgasmic coma, though.

Carmelo untied my wrists from the head board and they fell limp on top of my chest as I struggled to gain control of my breathing. I had cum so hard and so many times, the black silk sheets beneath me were soak and wet. He pulled me into his arms and kissed my ear as I slowly began to come down off of my erotic high.

"You good, Tavia?" he asked me in his sexy voice that could send my kitten in an uproar just hearing it.

I nodded my head. "Oh yeah," I said with a grin. He intertwined our fingers and kissed my ear again and before I knew it, I could tell he had fallen asleep by the sounds of his slow, deep breathing.

"Fuck!" I cursed myself. *"This mofo was not supposed to spend the night. That wasn't the plan. He was supposed to be moonwalking his ass to the 6 bus stop right now! Damn, I done fucked up again!"* I shook my head in disgust as I came to the realization that I had once again allowed this man's ability to fuck like a porn star trying to win a gold medal in the Hugh Hefner Olympics and eat pussy like a Cunnlingus king, lick his way into my heart, lick

Yani

his way into my bed… and lick me into submission. Shame on it all!

<u>Coming Summer 2016</u>